Winter will be over soon and we have new books guaranteed to put a spring in your step! Lose yourself in an absorbing read from Harlequin Presents....

Travel to sophisticated European locations and meet sexy foreign men. In *The Greek's Chosen Wife* by Lynne Graham, see what happens when gorgeous Greek Nikolas Angelis decides to make his convenient marriage real. *The Mancini Marriage Bargain* by Trish Morey is the conclusion of her exciting duet, THE ARRANGED BRIDES—we brought you the first book, *Stolen by the Sheikh*, last month.

Fly to more distant lands for Sandra Marton's UNCUT story, *The Desert Virgin.* Feel the heat as ruthless troubleshooter Cameron Knight rescues innocent ballerina Leanna DeMarco. If you haven't read an UNCUT story before, watch out—they're almost too hot to handle!

If you like strong men, you'll love our new miniseries RUTHLESS. This month in *The Billionaire Boss's Forbidden Mistress* by Miranda Lee, a boss expects his new receptionist to fall at his feet, and is surprised to find she's more of a challenge than he thought. Lucy Monroe's latest story, *Wedding Vow of Revenge*, promises scenes of searing passion and a gorgeous hero.

The Royal Marriage by Fiona Hood-Stewart is a classic tale of a young woman who has been promised in marriage to a royal prince. Only she's determined not to be ruled by him and her declaration of independence begins in the bedroom!

We hope you enjoy reading this month's selection. Look out for brand-new books next month!

We've captured a slice of royal
life in our miniseries

By Royal Command

Kings, counts, dukes and princes...

Don't miss these stories of charismatic kings,
commanding counts, demanding dukes and
playboy princes. Read all about their privileged
lives, love affairs...even their scandals!

Let us treat you like a queen—
relax and enjoy our regal miniseries.

Look out for more stories in this
miniseries—coming soon!

April 2006
The Italian Duke's Wife
by Penny Jordan
#2529

Fiona Hood-Stewart

THE ROYAL MARRIAGE

By Royal Command

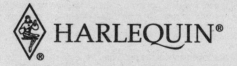
HARLEQUIN®

TORONTO • NEW YORK • LONDON
AMSTERDAM • PARIS • SYDNEY • HAMBURG
STOCKHOLM • ATHENS • TOKYO • MILAN • MADRID
PRAGUE • WARSAW • BUDAPEST • AUCKLÀND

ISBN 0-373-12527-5

THE ROYAL MARRIAGE

First North American Publication 2006.

Copyright © 2006 by Fiona Hood-Stewart.

www.eHarlequin.com

Printed in U.S.A.

All about the author...
Fiona Hood-Stewart

Born in Scotland and brought up internationally, Fiona went to boarding school in Switzerland, and then to several European universities. When Fiona married, she moved to South America where she ran her own design business before turning to fashion, for which she created her own label and opened several boutiques in Brazil and the U.S.

However, like the characters in her novels, Fiona has always been mystically drawn back to Scotland. In fact her family home served as the inspiration for Dunbar in her MIRA novel *The Journey Home.* She is well acquainted with all the locales that are visited in all her novels, which she infuses with her own life experiences. As she speaks seven languages fluently, Fiona has a unique insight and exposure into customs and lifestyles of foreign countries.

Fiona divides her time between Europe and her ranch in Brazil. She has two sons and travels frequently to Paris, New York and can be seen at the races in Deauville in France, or at Royal Ascot in the U.K.

Fiona credits her mother with putting her on the path to becoming a writer. "My mother always read aloud to me as a child. She didn't approve of television and I spent many hours with my nose in a book. As a child I read everything I could get my hands on."

CHAPTER ONE

As the four-by-four SUV raced over a bumpy road in the arid north-eastern Brazilian countryside, HRH Prince Ricardo of Maldoravia asked himself—not for the first time—what had induced him to accept an invitation that could only lead to trouble.

He glanced at the SUV's driver—a small, wiry individual in designer sunglasses, brown as a nut, with a wide smile and an attitude when it came to dealing with the local police. They seemed to enjoy stopping a car on the road for no apparent purpose other than to check papers, then hum and ha for a while, before sending its occupants on their way. Ricardo then glanced at his watch: three-thirty-five. The intense heat outside had penetrated the interior of the SUV, despite its tinted windows and the air-conditioning, which was on full blast. From his limited Portuguese, he understood the journey would take at least another hour. And that, he realised, could signify anything: time here had a different meaning.

He leaned back and stretched his legs as far as they would go. He must, he concluded wryly, be crazy to have accepted his late father's old friend's invitation. Gonzalo Guimaraes and his parent had studied together at Eton and Oxford many years ago, and although their lives had taken very different routes— Ricardo's father becoming ruler of the small island Principality of Maldoravia in the Mediterranean, and

Gonzalo heading back to his vast Brazilian *fazenda*—
the two men had enjoyed a lifelong friendship. And in
all those years Ricardo had never known Gonzalo to
ask for any favours. Which was what made the request
for Ricardo to visit him in his fiefdom all the more
intriguing.

They were driving along the coastline now, and the
landscape had changed: rolling waves, white sand and
scattered coconut trees swayed with samba-like
rhythm in the summer breeze. Two skimpily dressed
men sat by the roadside, seemingly oblivious to the
blazing sun. Another led a packed mule at a gentle
pace. Speed was apparently not a factor in this part of
the world. At one point Ricardo could see a little
bronzed boy of about ten holding up a snake with the
hopes of selling it to one of the few passers-by heading
along the dust-bitten road.

So, although he had misgivings about the trip,
Ricardo was fascinated. It was not the first time he'd
visited Brazil—he'd made a brief visit to Rio a few
years ago, for Carnival. But what he was seeing here
and now was a very different country, one locked in
a time warp where not much had changed and where
the outside world meant little.

An hour and a half later they turned left down an
earth road and the driver pointed to huge gates surrounded by coconut trees. Beyond them Ricardo spied
a small bridge. Thick vegetation hid whatever else lay
beyond. At the gates several dark-suited guards came
out and greeted them. One bowed and, through gold
teeth and in broken English, bade him welcome. Then
the gates opened electronically and the vehicle pro-
ceeded at a more sober pace up a driveway bordered
by a vivid mass of multi-coloured hibiscus and bou-

gainvillaea. To the right more coconut trees framed the cerulean ocean. The driveway, Ricardo noted, was in considerably better repair than the highway.

About a mile and a half farther on a sprawling mansion came into view—a maze of whitewashed walls and low-lying red-tiled roofs emerging from a panoply of lush vegetation. It was strangely harmonious, as though the architect had felt entirely in tune with his surroundings.

'We here,' Lando, the driver, proclaimed triumphantly as he stamped on the brakes and the SUV came to a standstill. Ricardo smiled thankfully. He wondered why Gonzalo didn't have a private airstrip, which would have made life a lot easier; he could certainly afford it.

Then servants appeared, doors opened, and as Ricardo exited the vehicle he saw Gonzalo, a man of medium height, brown and wiry—rather like the SUV's driver—in a short-sleeved white shirt and beige trousers, his thick white hair swept back, coming down some shallow steps to greet him.

'My friend,' he said, with a broad smile of greeting, 'welcome to my home.'

'Thank you. I'm happy to be here.' The two men shook hands warmly.

'I'm sorry we couldn't send the plane to pick you up in Recife, but there has been a problem with our radar system and in this back-of-beyond place we have to wait two days for the specialist to arrive. Usually my own team can take care of minor problems, but I'm afraid this time it was too complex. Come in out of the heat,' Gonzalo insisted.

Ricardo obeyed gladly and stepped inside a huge

cool marble hall. 'It certainly is hot out there,' he re-marked.

'At least forty degrees today,' Gonzalo agreed, lead-ing the way into a vast living room decorated with modern white sofas, Persian rugs, exotic plants and tasteful antiques. The panoramic view over the ocean was magnificent.

'You have a beautiful place here,' Ricardo said, gazing out, impressed. There was something wild and untamed about the landscape—something he couldn't define but that he found viscerally disturbing.

The two men sat down on the sofas and two uni-formed maids materialised with coffee and fruit juice.

'This fruit is *umbu*,' Gonzalo said as Ricardo tasted the refreshing juice. 'It is typical of the north-east of the country. We have a great variety of fruit here.'

'Delicious.' Ricardo was still wondering what it was that had triggered Gonzalo's urgent message. He was travelling incognito, having left his usual retinue be-hind in Maldoravia, and he was enjoying the freedom this allowed him. Right now he was content to bide his time. So, instead of showing overt curiosity as to why Gonzalo had summoned him, he sipped his juice and waited. Three years as ruler of the Principality had taught him patience. He had no doubt that all would be revealed in good time.

Several minutes later Gonzalo was conducting him up a wide marble staircase, past walls covered with bright colourful paintings that Gonzalo explained were from local and other South American artists, to a large suite of rooms. There the maids were already unpack-ing his belongings.

'I suggest you take a rest,' Gonzalo said. 'When it is cooler we can meet for drinks downstairs and chat.'

'That sounds perfect,' Ricardo replied.

A few minutes later he was under the shower, enjoying the rush of ice-cold water. When he got out he sleeked back his dark hair and twisted a bath towel around his waist. He was a tall, well-built man. At thirty-three, several years of working out had left him with a trim, sculpted body. His dark brown eyes surveyed the reflection of his finely chiselled face in the bathroom mirror as he debated whether he needed another shave.

Water still trickled down his tanned back as he moved across the marble floor towards French windows and opened the doors. As he stepped out onto the balcony he was met by a pleasant breeze. The scorching heat of earlier in the day had subsided. Leaning on the balustrade, he looked out towards the rolling sand dunes and the bright blue sea, intrigued. From here, the next port of call, he reflected thoughtfully, was Africa. There was clarity and luminosity now that the heat haze had subsided, leaving the coconut trees and the rich vegetation distinct.

Ricardo stretched. He was about to turn back inside and lie down when a movement in the far distance caught his eyes. Shading them from the setting sun, he watched a straight-backed female figure astride a handsome white horse approaching along the beach at a gentle canter. It made a pleasant picture. As she drew closer he could make out her lithe movements, and her long dark hair flowing wildly in the wind. The woman and the animal blended as though they were one.

Ricardo stood glued to the spot, watching as she reined the horse in, then dismounted easily onto the sand and shook her hair back. The horse stood obediently as she removed her jeans and shirt, revealing long bronzed limbs and a perfectly proportioned body encased in a tiny white bikini. Then, like a top model on a Parisian catwalk, she glided towards the water and entered the spray, dipped under a wave and then emerged. He could hear her laughing and calling to the horse. A smile broke on his lips as the animal trotted into the water and together they frolicked. It was a magical scene, unreal. A beautiful deserted landscape, a girl and a horse so in tune with one another. Like something out of a movie.

He wondered who she was. He knew little about Gonzalo's family—only that he had been a widower for many years. He had never met any of Gonzalo's children. Certainly he had never heard his own father mention any.

He stood straighter and observed the girl lead the horse out of the water, back to where she'd left her clothes. Even at this distance it was confirmed to him that her figure was almost perfect, and he experienced a rush of raw sexual attraction. Then, throwing her garments up on the horse, the girl leapt into the saddle.

Ricardo drew in his breath as she galloped off into the rich crimson sunset.

'You must naturally be wondering why I asked you to come here at a moment's notice,' Gonzalo remarked as, later, the two men sat on the lushly decorated veranda, which was furnished with dark rattan chairs upholstered with comfortable white cushions, low coffee tables and tropical plants.

It was pleasantly cool now. A gentle breeze blew in from the sea and a delicate crescent moon shone above them at a right angle. Night had fallen quickly due, Ricardo knew, to the proximity of the Equator.

Brightly etched stars dotted the inky sky even though it was still early. He could even distinguish the Southern Cross.

'I must confess to curiosity,' he said, taking a sip of whisky, studying his host.

'Then I shall not beat about the bush,' Gonzalo replied, with a wise, knowing smile that held a touch of sadness. 'I am an old man, Ricardo, and unfortunately my health is not in the best of shape.'

'I'm sorry to hear it.'

'So am I. Not for myself, you understand, but for one that I must leave behind when the time comes to pass on.'

'I wasn't aware that you were married.'

'I'm not now. I have been a widower for many years. I had no children from my first marriage. But years ago I had an affair with a young woman—a young English film star whose movie I financed. We were married in secret, as she didn't want the publicity to affect her career, but she was killed in a plane crash just two months after our daughter was born.'

Ricardo said nothing, merely crossed one leg over his knee and waited. Some favour was about to be asked, he was sure.

'Last month my doctors in New York told me that I have less than a year to live. It's cancer, I'm afraid, and it's terminal. I have only a few months left.'

'I'm deeply sorry,' Ricardo said, truly sad for his father's old friend. 'What can I do to help?'

Gonzalo took his time, swivelled his glass in his fingers, then looked Ricardo straight in the eye. 'Marry my daughter.'

'Excuse me?' Ricardo sat straighter. He had expected a request—but hardly this.

'I would like you to consider marriage to my daughter. A marriage of convenience. It is not unusual in your world. The Maldoravian royal family have always had planned marriages, as far as I can gather.'

'Maybe, but—'

'Even your own parents' marriage was arranged, dear boy. And I gather a marriage of convenience was what your father had planned for you, was it not?'

'That's all very well,' Ricardo countered. 'But my father is dead and times have changed, Gonzalo. I lead my own life now.'

'And from all I've heard you are enjoying it very thoroughly,' Gonzalo replied with a touch of dry humour. 'But you are thirty-three years old, Ricardo, and the succession must be thought of. Is there anyone you would consider as a future wife?'

'Well, actually, I haven't got around to thinking of marriage yet,' Ricardo replied, a picture of Ambrosia, his exotic Mexican mistress, forming in his mind. He had no intention of giving her up, even though marriage would never come into it. 'There is still time ahead of me.'

'Perhaps. I am not asking you to change your lifestyle, merely to consider an arrangement that could be advantageous to both parties. After all, you need an heir—and a wife who is both suitable socially and a virgin. Also, it has come to my knowledge,' Gonzalo added with a speculative look before Ricardo could interrupt, 'that your uncle Rolando has made some unfortunate deals for the Principality.'

This last was true. But how this knowledge, which had been kept very secret in the family, could have reached Gonzalo was beyond him. Ricardo experienced a twitch of irritation. Time to tread very carefully, he realised, on the alert now.

'There have been one or two unfortunate incidents,' he said guardedly, 'but nothing serious.'

'No. But I remember your father telling me that it is written in the Maldoravian constitution that until you marry you are still obliged to accept your uncle's participation in the Principality's government, aren't you? And, should you die without issue, he will automatically become ruler. A daunting thought,' Gonzalo murmured, letting his words sink in.

'That is true.' There was an edge of bitterness to Ricardo's voice. His uncle had been nothing but trouble with his profligate lifestyle. The fact that he was second in line to the throne was subtly brought home to Ricardo by his Cabinet on every possible occasion.

'What I propose,' Gonzalo continued smoothly, 'is a scheme that could help you organise your affairs satisfactorily and help me die in peace.'

'Gonzalo, I would love to help you, but—'

'Your father and I used to talk of this sometimes— jokingly, you understand. But now time is of the essence. My daughter, Gabriella, is nineteen. She will inherit my entire fortune—which, though I say it myself, is sizeable. I cannot leave her unprotected. I fear for her future. I would like to know that she will be marrying someone who will respect her and take care of her affairs, as I know you would. There would be many other advantages to the match, of course, but those we can discuss in due course.'

'I think I had better make it quite clear,' Ricardo replied coldly 'that I consider marriage a big step. I do not view it as a business arrangement, and I am afraid that I must therefore decline. If there is anything

I can do to help protect your daughter in other ways, then you can count on me. But I'm afraid marriage is out.'

Gonzalo smiled. 'I expected this reaction. It proves you are truly the kind of man I thought you had grown into. Your father's son. But enough for now. Let us relax and talk of other matters.'

At that moment the clipped echo of high heels on marble interrupted the conversation. Ricardo turned. Gonzalo's head flew up and a warm smile lit his eyes.

'*Querida,*' he said, rising, as did Ricardo. 'Come in and let me introduce you to His Royal Highness Prince Ricardo of Maldoravia.'

He was certainly handsome, even if he was quite old, Gabriella reflected as she glided into the room, eyeing Ricardo askance out of the corner of her eye. But she knew exactly what her father was up to and had no intention of co-operating. Why he had suddenly become fixed on marrying her off to someone when she had very different plans for her future was beyond her. She would let this man know exactly what she thought of the whole scheme. But for now she would play their game, get her own show on the road, and then, when the time came, she would twist her father round her little finger—as she always had.

'Ricardo—this is my daughter, Gabriella.'

Stopping in front of Ricardo, she extended long, tapered, tanned fingers. 'Good evening,' she said coolly. 'Welcome to the Fazenda Boa Luz.'

'Good evening.' Ricardo spontaneously raised her fingers to his lips, recognising Gabriella as the girl he'd seen earlier on the beach. He had rarely beheld a more beautiful young woman. She carried herself with such grace and elegance that it was difficult to believe someone so young could have acquired this kind of poise.

Gabriella sat down gracefully next to her father. Her flimsy white spaghetti-strapped chiffon dress emphasised the delicate curves of her slim, sinuous body. The single diamond at her throat shone against her tanned skin. Her long black hair cascaded silkily to her waist and her large green eyes shone, but her straight, chiselled nose looked almost disdainful as she crossed her legs. The chiffon parted, revealing never-ending limbs. She was a picture of studied elegance.

Ricardo wondered if she knew of her father's plan. There was a proud, rebellious glint in her eye that reminded him of the rolling waves and untamed natural beauty he'd observed earlier in the day. Another rush of heat gripped him. He took a long sip of whisky and disguised the desire that had sparked within him.

Just as conversation was about to resume, a uniformed servant appeared. 'There is a call for you from Brasilia in the study, Seu Gonzalo,' he murmured to his master.

'Ah, yes. Will you excuse me?' Gonzalo got up and disappeared through the wide double doors.

Ricardo and Gabriella sat in silence. She made no effort to engage him in conversation, simply smiled at the servant as he placed a flute of champagne before her on the low coffee table.

'Do you live here all year round?' Ricardo asked at last, letting his eyes course lazily over her. This girl was far too confident for her own good.

'No. I travel and study. I was at school in Switzerland until six months ago.'

'I see. What do you plan to study?'

'There is no need for you to make polite conversation with me,' she replied, her gaze haughty. Her English was perfect, except for a slight sexy lilt. 'I know exactly why you are here and I despise you for it.' Her eyes blazed suddenly like two glittering emeralds.

'You do?' Ricardo raised an amused brow, intrigued by her candour.

'Yes. You have come here to inspect me, as you might a filly, because Father wants you to marry me. I don't know why he has taken this idea into his head, but you could have saved yourself the trouble of your journey. I find it rather amusing that you should travel halfway across the world on a fool's errand.'

'You don't say?' Ricardo's voice was smoothly sardonic. His brow rose once more and he leaned back against the cushions, preparing to enjoy himself. Both beautiful and amusing. And in need of a sharp lesson. Had he been at home in his palazzo, his retinue would have rolled their eyes, aware of the danger signs. HRH was charming, but when crossed...

'Yes,' Gabriella continued obliviously. 'My advice to you is that you tell him right away that you don't agree to the plan. It'll make this so much simpler for all of us.' She took a long sip of champagne, sat back languidly on the sofa and flicked an invisible speck of dust from the skirt of her dress.

'Then you will be glad to know that I already have,' Ricardo replied smoothly, masking his amusement.

'You did?' The sophisticated camouflage dropped for a few surprised seconds, and he watched, intrigued, as her pride wobbled and the wind was neatly taken out of her sails.

'Yes. Like you, I find the whole idea of a planned

marriage with a stranger intolerable, and I entirely agree that it is far better to scotch any illusions your father may have right away. I'm glad we both feel the same way,' he added with a warm smile.

'Uh, yes, of course. But didn't you know why he'd asked you to come?'

'Actually, no. I only learned the reason a few minutes ago. But don't worry. I made quite sure there could be no doubt as to my reply. I have no desire to get married. Much less to an unknown nineteen-year-old,' he finished lazily.

Gabriella seethed inwardly. How dared he talk to her like this? She sent him back a bright brittle smile that revealed a row of perfect white teeth. 'That's wonderful. I'm so glad we see things eye to eye. Lucky, isn't it?'

'Isn't it? So, you see, now we can relax and you can tell me all about this place. After all, as you so rightly pointed out, I have came all this way on a wild goose chase, and I might as well spend a few days getting to know the region. I've never been to this part of Brazil before.'

'Naturally you must stay,' Gabriella replied, quickly retrieving her poise, once again the perfect hostess.

This man, she realised uncomfortably, was nothing like the picture she'd created in her imaginative mind. He was neither fat nor ugly, nor did he leer. Well, actually, she'd known that already, from having read about him in glossy magazines. But still. Not only was he devastatingly and disturbingly handsome, but there was something about him that attracted her in a way she'd never experienced before.

And he had the nerve to make it quite clear he wasn't interested in her!

That had never happened before. Since her early childhood Gabriella Guimaraes had been brought up to consider herself a rare beauty, a wealthy heiress, and a great catch. It came as a disconcerting blow to realise he was watching her rather as he might an amusing puppy. Well, that would not last long, she determined. A glint entered her emerald-tinted eyes as she leaned forward to reach for her glass, making sure she revealed a little more bronzed leg. He might not want to marry her, but she would make damn sure he knew exactly who he was dealing with. Gabriella Guimaraes was used to crooking her finger and watching all the young men she knew crawl, drooling, at her feet. She was not about to see that change.

Prince or no Prince.

CHAPTER TWO

THE horses moved abreast of one another, one white, one chestnut, galloping across the wet sand and kicking up a spray as they raced along the beach towards the setting sun, which was etched like a stark ball of fire on the pink horizon.

Ricardo had spent a pleasant day driving around the estate with Gonzalo. Then they'd returned for a late lunch of *ensopado de camarao*, a delicious dish of shrimp stew prepared with coconut milk, accompanied by white rice, black beans and *farofa*—a preparation of manioc flour and butter—and washed down with a Caipirinha—sugar cane alcohol with crushed lime and ice.

Then, after a siesta, Gonzalo had suggested Ricardo and Gabriella take a ride.

'Take your swimming shorts,' Gonzalo had said to Ricardo, 'and you can have a swim—either in the ocean or at the *cachoeira*. Gabriella will show you. She goes there regularly.'

And now here they were, galloping along the ocean's edge, the scent of the sea filling their nostrils, a soft wind caressing their skin.

'Follow me.' Gabriella twisted around in her saddle and called out suddenly. Then, changing direction, she headed up the beach and galloped inland, towards a tropical landscape of heavy vegetation that reminded

21

him of the rainforest. Soon they were moving at a slower pace along a path through a maze of tropical trees interspersed with glimmers of red sunlight. Ricardo followed, watching the slim figure in the saddle before him, her hair catching the glinting light.

Then, when he least expected it, the thick vegetation gave way and they rode into a clearing. To his surprise Ricardo saw a small natural lake, at the far end of which a waterfall cascaded over stark rocks into silent dark green waters. It was extraordinarily beautiful.

'Isn't it lovely?' Gabriella exclaimed proudly, leaping off her horse. 'This is where we'll swim.'

'It's amazing,' Ricardo agreed, following suit and leaving his horse to graze as she had, watching her as once again she slipped off her clothes. He stood a moment appreciating the view: her body was spectacular, bronzed and smooth, her limbs long and lithe, her yellow bikini tiny. Yet there was nothing provocative in her stance. She was graceful and sexy, yet he got the impression she was not fully aware of just how sexy she actually was. He took a deep breath, then removed his own jeans and joined her at the water's edge.

Gabriella flashed him a quick, challenging smile. 'Race you to the other side,' she said, diving expertly in.

With no hesitation Ricardo followed. They were head-to-head when he realised Gabriella was an excellent swimmer. But soon he was several strokes ahead, and waiting for her when she reached the other side.

Her head emerged from the water, hair sleeked

back, eyes flashing. Ricardo grinned wickedly as they faced one another. A rush of desire coursed through him as she stood with the water barely reaching her hips, arched, then sank and dipped her head back in the water again, revealing the perfect curve of her small, firm breasts.

'You're not a bad swimmer for a prince,' she remarked with a pout as she straightened up again.

'What has my being a prince got to do with my swimming abilities?' He laughed, watching as she waded into even shallower water, her movements emphasising the curves of her exquisite figure.

'Nothing.' She shrugged, laughing too. 'I just thought that a prince would stay in a stuffy palace and be terribly correct. You don't seem prince-like at all.'

'Well, I'm glad I've restored your faith in princes,' Ricardo replied, amused. 'I do that too—being correct and stuffy, I mean—but not right now.' Instinctively he moved closer to her, the desire to touch her, to feel that delicious skin and that body in his arms overwhelming.

'I imagined you differently,' she said, sinking into the water and floating on her back.

'Really? How?'

'Well, you are quite old, of course, so I thought you'd be more serious. Hey, I'm going to stand under the waterfall. Want to come?'

'Why not?' Together they moved towards the rush of water. 'Usually I swim naked here,' she said with a touch of regret. 'It feels great.'

'Don't let me inhibit you.'

She moved from under the spray and looked at him

speculatively, her eyes filled with haughty challenge and a touch of doubt. Then she tossed her head and sent him a challenging glare. 'Okay. Hold on to this for me, will you?' Wriggling provocatively under the water, which barely covered her breasts, she slipped off the brief bikini and handed it to him. Then, before he could react, she was swimming away—a lissome, bewitching mermaid, playing a nimble game of hide-and-seek in the deep dark waters.

Ricardo watched her, fascinated, desire clouding his reason. Without hesitation he removed his swimming shorts. Tossing them to where Gabriella's bikini lay, he swam after her, catching her waist and turning her abruptly about.

'This is a dangerous game you're playing, little girl,' he murmured, his voice husky with pent-up desire as he drank in her full parted lips, her challenging yet hesitant eyes, her laughing head thrown back. But as his arms came around her he felt her stiffen, saw her sea-green eyes turn dark with doubt.

But it was too late.

Before she could move he drew her more firmly into his arms, felt the soft curve of her breast meet his hard chest, heard the quick indrawn breath. Instinctively his hands glided down her back. His cupped her firm, beautifully curved bottom and pressed her closer against him, until she felt the hardness of his desire. He saw her lips part in surprise, felt her gesture of restraint, saw the doubt in her eyes and knew he should stop. Instead his lips came down on hers, parting, seeking, provoking a soft yet anxious response as expertly he kissed her.

Gabriella had wanted to provoke him, but this was not at all the reaction she had expected. She had been kissed before—usually at a school dance—but had always found it boring. She was used to being in control, the one who decided when it would begin and when it would end. But now she was out of her league. She had never stood naked in a man's arms before, and as Ricardo's hand reached her breast she let out a gasp. She had never meant for anything like this to occur. Yet it was so new, so wonderful, so delicious, so incredibly sensual that all she could do was wind her arms about his neck and feel, letting her body cleave to his. It was an incredible sensation. Never had she been so close to a man. She knew she was the one who had sought the situation and that it was too late to draw back, even had she wanted to.

They kissed again. The movement of the water had brought them back beneath the rushing waterfall. Gabriella gasped as his thumb grazed her taut, aching nipples and her body arched with a new and pounding desire. She let out a tiny cry of delight as he played with her, slowly, expertly, drawing something from deep inside her that she couldn't describe, it travelled so deep. Then his fingers coursed down, seeking between her thighs, and she drew back, breathless.

'No,' she murmured, swallowing, catching her breath and shaking her head as she broke out of his arms.

Their eyes met—his clouded with desire, hers sparkling with new sensations mixed with misgiving.

'Gabriella, you wanted this,' Ricardo murmured, reaching his hand out and drawing her back towards him, thinking in the back of his mind that her father obviously had false illusions about her if he believed she was a virgin.

'I—I… No. We mustn't.' She shook her head again, let her fingers course down his chest and let out a sigh.

'Why not? You were obviously enjoying yourself,' he said, with a touch of arrogant masculine pride.

'My father would kill us.'

He looked down into her eyes, drowning there. His hands returned to her breasts and he caught her short gasp. 'You want this as much as I do. Don't deny it,' he muttered, slipping his fingers between her thighs and drawing her back into his arms.

She was delicious, the most delicious woman he had known for years. Only in his very early youth had he experienced the range of sensations that gripped him now. Lifting her legs around his waist, he felt her arms encircle his neck, saw her lips part and her wet skin shining as their shadows reflected in the still water. Her eyes were filled with longing and her breasts peaked with unrepentant longing. It was too much to resist. Guiding himself, he'd prepared to thrust inside her when she let out a sharp cry. Immediately he stopped and withdrew. But, catching her waist, he pulled her back to him.

'I—I can't,' she cried, turning her head away. 'I've never—I…'

'Why didn't you tell me that you were a virgin?' Ricardo asked, his expression dark with anger.

'I…' She swallowed, looked away again, then tilted her chin, her proud profile stubborn. She shrugged.

'I am not in the habit of deflowering virgins,' he

snapped. His hands dropped and he moved away to the wake's edge. Leaping out, he dressed quickly and mounted his horse. 'If this is the way you behave with men, I would counsel you to be more careful. One day you may come across someone who isn't quite as controlled as I am.' With that he wheeled his horse around, leaving Gabriella standing in the water.

She let out a ragged sigh. What had she been thinking of? She felt a rush of tears surface. It was all so difficult. Her father was determined that she should marry—that she shouldn't go to model in London, as she wanted to. Her whole life was a mess. And now this man, whom she'd been so determined to reject, was turning out to be the most enticing, attractive being she'd ever met. It wasn't fair.

Lifting herself out of the water, she sat for a moment on the edge of the pool, then reached shakily for her bikini on the grass. How could she have been so brazen as to take off her clothes in front of him and allow this to happen? She closed her eyes and felt a rush of heat suffuse her face. He must despise her—think that she was an easy lay. Or at the very least a tease, now that he knew she was a virgin.

Slowly Gabriella got up, whistled to Belleza, her horse, threw her clothes up over the saddle and mounted reluctantly. By now Ricardo would be almost back at the house. What would he do? Tell her father? No, probably not. But how would she face him at dinner? It was all so embarrassing. And, to make it worse, the whole thing was her own fault.

Letting out a deep huff, she rode slowly back to the beach and headed for home.

*   *   *

He could hardly leave tonight, Ricardo concluded, but tomorrow morning he would make a reasonable excuse and be on his way. The situation had got out of hand. He should have known she was a child playing with fire, and he blamed his own rush of passion for what had happened. She hadn't known what she was doing. But it was hard to forget her natural instinctive reaction—the hot, charismatic longing that had vibrated between them. As he showered, Ricardo tried to clear his mind and think reasonably. It was just physical, nothing more, he reminded himself as he dressed for dinner.

Gabriella dressed carefully, choosing a pale blue designer shift that fitted perfectly, all chiffon and lace, bought on her last trip to Milan, and thin, high-heeled satin sandals to match. Instead of leaving her hair loose she brushed it back in a strict ponytail that left her elegant rather than sexy. Diamonds sparkled in her ears. Taking a deep breath, she took a last look in the mirror then headed downstairs to face what would inevitably be an embarrassing encounter.

Ricardo rose as she entered the living room. She glanced at him sideways, unsure of his reaction. But to her surprise he acted as if the afternoon's interlude had never taken place. Gabriella experienced a rush of gratitude. She let out a tiny sigh of relief and sat next to her father, taking his hand in hers and giving him a hug. It felt secure to be next to him, to know he would always protect her, whatever happened in her life.

'So, my love,' Gonzalo said fondly, patting her cheek, 'did you two have a nice afternoon?'

'Very pleasant, thank you,' she answered demurely.

Ricardo watched her, resisting the desire to smile. She was a piece of work, he realised, amused despite his anger at her foolish behaviour. She was very young, and perhaps she had over-estimated herself— had no idea of just how patently sexy she was. He found himself feeling indulgent towards her as she cuddled next to her father, looking much younger despite her sophisticated outfit and the ponytail.

Dinner was announced and they rose. Then suddenly Gonzalo stopped, lifted his hand to his chest.

'Daddy?' Gabriella held him, sending Ricardo a panicked look. 'What's wrong, Daddy?' she cried.

Ricardo rushed to the other man's side, saw his face turn white. 'We must lie him down on the couch immediately,' he said, taking Gonzalo's weight and laying him among the cushions.

'Daddy, what's wrong?' Gabriella cried, grabbing her father's hand.

Gonazalo's eyes closed and his breath came fast. Then his lips opened. 'Promise me,' he whispered in a weak voice. 'Give me your hand,' he said to Ricardo.

Ricardo frowned and took the old man's hand, felt him place it over Gabriella's. 'I am leaving you, little one,' he whispered. 'I want you both to promise that you will marry within a month.'

Gabriella's eyes flew in panic from her father to Ricardo.

'But you can't go—you can't leave me, Papa,' she cried, panic-stricken, tears pouring down her cheeks.

It was a split-second decision. But as Ricardo looked from father to daughter, saw the anguish in the dying man's eyes, the lost distress in the girl's, he knew there was no choice.

'I promise,' he said, loud and clear.

'My Gabinha,' the old man whispered, his voice weaker by the moment. 'Answer me.'

'I—Daddy, don't leave me,' Gabriella wept.

'Promise me, my darling.'

'I…I promise,' she whispered, her head falling.

Ricardo watched as Gonzalo let out his last breath and Gabriella, her hair splayed over his chest, wept uncontrollably. A few minutes elapsed before slowly he lifted her and held her silently in his arms, aware that he had just made the biggest commitment—and perhaps the biggest mistake—of his life.

CHAPTER THREE

'WE CAN'T get married,' Gabriella insisted, not for the first time. 'It's absurd. We were under pressure. Daddy can't have meant it. He was just—' She cut herself off and turned away.

It was three weeks now since Gonzalo's funeral, and they were on Ricardo's private plane, a G5, flying to the Principality of Maldoravia, which he'd virtually abandoned for the past month. He needed to decide what the next step was. Not an easy task, he reflected, glancing at Gabriella, who had lived through the past weeks' events in a daze, allowing him to take charge of both her personal and business arrangements.

They had spent several days in the Presidential suite at the Copacabana Palace Hotel in Rio while Ricardo went over all Gonzalo's personal affairs with the lawyers and trustees appointed to administer them—only to discover that he was bound to Gabriella by the terms of Gonzalo's will. Sly old dog, he'd clearly known he'd get his way! Gabriella had sat by, barely registering what was happening, too caught up in her grief to care. He'd felt deeply sorry for her, and worried too. Her life had changed at the flick of a switch. It couldn't be easy, he recognised. She had lost quite a bit of weight too, he noted, eyeing her in the opposite seat and wondering how to get her to eat more than a couple of forkfuls of lettuce. Still, the subject at hand had to be faced.

'Gabriella, like it or not, we made a promise to a dying man. We must keep our word.'

'It was emotional blackmail,' she argued, crossing her arms tightly across her chest. 'It's not fair on either of us.'

'Nevertheless, I would not be a man of honour if I did not keep my word,' Ricardo said with a sigh. They'd had this discussion several times in the past days.

'That's rubbish and you know it. You could very well take care of my affairs and leave it at that.'

'You read the will yourself,' he said wearily. 'You can receive nothing—no income, or any part of your inheritance—until our marriage has taken place. Why not make it easier on yourself? Or is the prospect of marrying me really such a dreadful one?' He raised a brow and looked at her, an amused gleam flashing in his dark eyes.

'It's not you,' she said looking away. 'It's that I don't want to marry anyone. Not yet, anyway. I'm nineteen. I want to live. Not be tied down by a husband.'

Despite her unflattering words Ricardo sympathised with her, and wished as he had several times over the past few weeks that the dramatic circumstances of Gonzalo's imminent death hadn't changed his life and hers. But they had, and it was too late to retract.

'I understand how you feel,' he said matter-of-factly, 'but the fact remains that we have to get married, Gabriella. I gave my word and so did you. There are also the terms of your father's will. What happens after that is a different matter.'

'What do you mean?' she asked, frowning.

'Well, what I meant was that we can find a solution for this marriage which will allow us to live together without—how can I put this…?' He was already regretting his words. 'Without being a burden on one another.'

'Perhaps you could explain better,' she said, her eyes narrowing. 'I'm afraid I don't quite get the picture.'

'No. Well, never mind. I hope to make you very happy,' he answered quickly.

'No, you don't.' She shook her head vigorously and leaned forward, her eyes ablaze. 'I know exactly what you want. I've seen it over and over with my father's friends. You want to marry me, make me have a bunch of children, and then, while I sit in your wretched palace, taking care of them, you'll be off having fun with beautiful sexy girls. Do you think I'm stupid?' she said, hair flying as she rose and whirled to face him. 'Do you think that I don't know how men like you live? That my father was a saint and didn't have a bunch of mistresses all half his age? Well, I have news for you, Your Royal Highness. I am not going to be subjected to the kind of arrangement you—and obviously my father too—seem to think right for me. I have other plans for my life, and they don't include becoming a brood mare.'

'I never said that,' Ricardo replied, astounded at the onslaught. He'd expected opposition, but hardly this.

'But you implied it,' she spat.

'No, I didn't,' he replied through gritted teeth. 'I happen to take the commitment of marriage very seriously. And neither do I want an unwilling bride.'

'Then don't marry me,' she flashed. 'It's as simple as that.'

'I am responsible for all your affairs now. I have told the trustees of your inheritance that we will marry as agreed. Believe me,' he added, an edge to his voice, 'I have as little desire to go through with this damn wedding as you apparently have.'

'Thanks,' she said, flopping back in the seat, her eyes still glinting. Crossing her arms angrily, she stared out of the window at the clouds.

'Gabriella, do not try my patience any further. I have tried to be of as much solace to you as possible over the past weeks. But frankly you are being impossible. Why not try and make the best of the situation? We'll manage somehow.'

'Oh? Is that what you think?' Her eyes blazed again as she let out a ragged breath and her lip trembled. 'I've lost the only man I ever cared for. Life will never be the same without my father. But you can't understand that, I suppose?'

'Of course I understand,' Ricardo replied, his tone softening as he leaned forward to take her hand. 'I know this has been all very unexpected and traumatic for you. But why not make the best of the situation instead of the worst? This is a marriage of convenience, after all. I'm not asking for more than you're prepared to give—merely for you to comply with what we have both committed to.'

Gabriella shrugged, swallowed, looked down at his

fingers covering hers and suppressed the thrill that rushed up her arm and coursed to the pit of her stomach. How could she tell him that it would be hell to be married to him knowing that he was only doing it for the sake of his word given to a dying man? That he affected her in a way no other man ever had? She shuddered, remembering, as she had more than once over the past weeks, that episode at the waterfall. Slowly she drew her hand away. 'I'll think about it.'

'Not for too long, I hope,' he replied dryly. 'The month comes to an end in five days. Unless we are married by then you will lose your entire inheritance. I have already put the wedding plans in motion. Your gown is being prepared as we speak, and tomorrow we shall have the first rehearsal. There will be a lot of protocol for you to learn in a very short time. After all, this will be a state occasion.'

'How could you?' she whispered, her eyes filling with tears. 'And Papa? He loved me so much—always gave me everything I wanted or asked for. How could he do this to me? Threaten to leave mc with nothing if I don't obey?'

'He is not leaving you with nothing, merely making sure that you are not taken advantage of,' Ricardo repeated for the umpteenth time. 'You are a very wealthy young woman, Gabriella.'

'That's a totally ridiculous, outmoded and chauvinistic way of looking at things,' she exclaimed. 'And you,' she added accusingly, '*you* think just the way he did—that because I'm young and a woman I'm incapable of dealing with my own affairs.'

'Actually, you're right, I do,' Ricardo replied

coolly, tired of arguing. 'Have it your own way, Gabriella. But unless you want to remain penniless you had better get used to the idea of being married in three days' time. Anyway, I have made all the arrangements. The ceremony will take place in the Cathedral of Maldoravia on Thursday afternoon.'

'And what if I refuse?'

'Then you'll have no choice but to go out into the world on your own, without any visible means of support, and I shall inherit your entire fortune,' he said bluntly, hoping it would have the right effect.

'Well, that's fine. If you feel quite happy with that then go ahead. I don't want the damn money. Take it.' She jumped up from her seat and glared down at him. 'I don't care about the fortune. I'll go to London and model and make a fortune of my own. I—'

'Gabriella, have you the slightest notion of how many girls try to model, and what the percentage is of those who actually succeed? Not many, I assure you. Now, sit down and stop carrying on like a spoiled brat.'

'I am not a spoiled brat,' she spat. 'I have rights.'

'Well, unless you comply with my arrangements— and the terms of your father's will—as of Saturday morning those rights fly straight out the window,' he said, in a firm, cold voice that sent shivers down her spine. 'I assure you, Gabriella, that if you do not behave properly I will not lift one finger to assist you.'

'Oh! How could you?' she threw at him, trembling, her hair thrown back and her eyes the colour of emeralds. 'I hate you, Ricardo. I really loathe and detest you.'

'Well, that bodes well,' he muttered, picking up a financial magazine and leaning back in the wide leather seat while Gabriella stomped off to the other end of the plane to nurse her temper.

The following couple of days were filled with activity. From the moment she set foot in Maldoravia Gabriella was taken in hand by personal assistants, servants, and Ricardo's charming aunt, the Contessa Elizabetta. She barely saw Ricardo, but although she felt rather lost and forlorn, she also could not help being excited at all the preparations taking place. There were fittings for her wedding gown, her trousseau, her going-away outfit—all of which she tried hard to seem uninterested in. But her innate sense of and love for fashion made that difficult.

On Wednesday afternoon she sat with the Contessa and her new personal assistant Sara—an Englishwoman of thirty, who had been hired at the last minute for her efficiency and for the fact that she had worked at Buckingham Palace and at several other royal establishments and knew the ropes. Gabriella had eyed her suspiciously at first, and said that she didn't need an assistant. But with supreme tact and charm Sara had won her over. Now both the older women exchanged glances and the Contessa raised her brows as Gabriella stared out of the window and for the thousandth time expressed her views.

'It's just not fair. I don't know how he can do it. And to say he'd simply inherit my money and be done with it. I mean, can you imagine?'

'I think Ricardo is merely trying to help you, my love,' the Contessa replied soothingly.

'Well, I don't care. Sara?' Gabriella said, turning round to face her assistant, who sat next to the Contessa wearing an elegant beige suit. 'Don't you think I could be a success as a model? I mean, look at me. I'm exotic, I'm tall enough, and I have all the right measurements,' she pleaded.

'Yes. But, you see, the trend at the moment in London is for sylph-like blondes. I'm afraid you might considered a little too…uh…' Sara searched for a suitable word '…too voluptuous. Perhaps in the future your look will return, and then you could consider it. In the meantime, if we could just go over tonight's seating arrangements?' she went on, producing a file and flipping through it. 'I think you would feel more at ease.'

Gabriella rolled her eyes and flopped into the nearest armchair. 'You really mean me to marry him, don't you?'

'Well, my dear, I don't see what other solution there is,' the Contessa said kindly, patting her coiffed silver hair with a bejewelled hand. 'After all, I can think of worse fates than being married to Ricardo.'

'I'm glad you can,' Gabriella muttered under her breath.

'He's very handsome—and quite a catch. I can think of all sorts of women who will be wild with jealousy,' the Contessa replied in an encouraging tone.

'Ah! You see! I knew it. Other women. That's precisely what I'm worried about. He says he wants a marriage of convenience,' Gabriella said, curling her

legs under her and leaning further back into the armchair. 'That means he will have all sorts of horrid mistresses and I shall be left to wither in this—' she
waved her hand expressively '—in this dungeon.'

'I would hardly call the Palazzo Maldoravia a dungeon,' Sara countered, hiding a smile. 'Your apartments are equipped with the finest furnishings, and the
Jacuzzi works wonderfully. I had it tested myself.'

'It might as well be a dungeon for all I care,'
Gabriella muttered.

Thursday dawned a beautiful sunny spring day. From
the windows of her rooms in the Palazzo, Gabriella
looked out at the perfect sky. The Mediterranean glit-
tered clear and blue below, like a magical pond.

And now what was she to do? she wondered, opening the French doors and moving towards the balustrade of the balcony. Her black hair blew in the light
morning breeze and the scent of jasmine filled her nostrils. At any other time she would have been enchanted. But right now the idyllic scene was lost on
her. For the first time in her life Gabriella Guimaraes
had come to the true realisation that she was not in
control of the situation—and that, more than anything
else, was driving her crazy.

. That, and the fact that she was deeply and danger-
ously attracted to her future husband and damned if
she would let him know it. What could be worse, she
wondered, than to marry a man you found devastatingly attractive when probably right now he was making love to another woman?

'Oooh,' Gabriella seethed, throwing her head back

as she clutched the stone parapet and stared at the sky. She would never abase herself, never forgo her pride, never give in to him, never, ever submit to the kind of humiliation she had seen too many women go through.

As her father's only daughter, she had accompanied him in adult circles from her earliest childhood. Very soon she had seen what too many women's plights were, had listened to confidences beyond her years and seen men she knew were married parading their beautiful mistresses in full view of society. Why, she would rather live in hell than become one of them! It was absurd. For, although he was always charming, she knew that Ricardo only treated her like that because he was too polite to do otherwise, that deep down she was nothing but a duty, an obligation to be dealt with, another piece of business to be resolved. It was too infuriating. Too humiliating for words.

She turned back towards the room, hands clenched, her well-manicured nails digging into her palms at the thought of Ricardo and his behaviour over the past weeks. He had been wonderful and kind and the best friend anyone could have wished for when her father died. And she appreciated that—was grateful. But that was how he thought of her. A little girl he was sorry for because she was alone in the world. An obligation he had to fulfil.

She had racked her brains to find a solution, had again tried to persuade him to change his mind about the wedding that was to take place later today. But in vain. Ricardo had merely admonished her to pay attention to the protocol that had been instilled into her from the moment she'd stepped foot in the Principality. She sighed, stared out at the sea again, and her shoulders slumped. For the first time in her life she felt defeated. Instead of an excited bride she resembled a young queen preparing to face the gallows.

'He might as well be a frog,' she muttered under her breath. But deep down she knew that was not quite true, that it was precisely his undeniable attraction that disturbed her. If she were truthful she would have to admit that she even felt a fondness for the man he had proved himself to be—found his virile presence next to her disturbing yet reassuring. And for some reason she could not feel quite at ease in his company—particularly as flashes of that swim at the waterfall kept haunting her imagination, leaving her weak and wanting in a way she had never experienced previously.

Determined to get a grip on herself, and not allow him to perceive any of her weaknesses, Gabriella turned again back into the room and headed for the shower. There was no use trying to delay things any longer. She would marry him because, for now, there was no other way out. But he would find that he had a wife to be reckoned with.

In his office downstairs in the Palace Ricardo was experiencing his own set of doubts. His councillors were actually pleased that he was embarking on matrimony. They'd often mentioned the succession, and hinted at how providing an heir as soon as possible would eliminate the possibility of his uncle Rolando ever becoming Prince. But Ricardo had no illusions about his marriage. It was not going to be easy. Gabriella had made it plain that she meant to be as uncooperative as possible.

He raised his brows and let out a sigh. If he had not been a man of honour he would most definitely have got out of the duty that Gonzalo had forced upon him. He had even studied all the clauses of the will to see if there was any out. But none had presented itself. There was nothing for it but to bite the bullet and go through with it. He just hoped that Gabriella would behave. He'd had her primed in all the etiquette by his aunt, Contessa Elizabetta, and by the efficient Sara Harvey, whom thankfully she had taken to.

The Contessa was attractive and sympathetic, and had listened to Gabriella's complaints—at the same time managing to prepare her for what was going to be a state occasion at very short notice. Gossip was rife, he realised ruefully. Everyone wondered if the young girl was pregnant. An amusing assumption under the circumstances, he reflected, pushing away the papers he'd been studying and getting up from behind the huge mahogany desk.

Pregnant. Ricardo almost laughed. There was nothing amorous in their relationship. Far from it. In fact he wondered how they were going to fare in that department. He had never come close to kissing her again, and the day by the waterfall was nothing but a distant memory.

But one that would not quite disappear.

Still, despite that one occasion, Gabriella had kept him at arm's length. This stuck in his craw. Most women found him devastatingly attractive. But

Gabriella had made it plain that she had no desire for any intimacy, and on the few occasions when he'd tried to get things on to a happier footing she had rejected him outright. He grimaced, then glanced at the message from Ambrosia, to which he still hadn't replied, and rose from behind the desk. He would deal with that problem in due course. Right now it was time to prepare for his wedding—hardly the moment to be ringing his mistress. The future would take care of itself. He could do no more than perform his duty.

The rest was up to fate.

'Gosh, you're absolutely beautiful!' Princess Constanza, Ricardo's attractive younger sister, had just arrived for the wedding with her husband, the handsome Count Wilhelm of Wiesthun, and their two enchanting young children, who were to be attendants at the ceremony.

Gabriella turned away from the mirror. She was standing still while the designer's assistants gave the finishing touches to her magnificent yet simple satin wedding dress, a confection from Paris. Despite her unease she smiled at the attractive young woman at the door, and the pretty children.

'Hello, hello.' Constanza wafted in, a chestnut-haired woman of twenty-eight in a chic pale pink satin designer suit. She went over and kissed Gabriella on both cheeks. 'I heard all about what happened. You poor, poor thing. I was so sorry to hear about your father. And now you're stuck with Ricardo,' she remarked, grimacing and flopping onto the chintz sofa. 'He can be perfectly odious—even though he's a super brother.'

Gabriella eyed her and smiled. 'Are those your children?' she asked, watching the two little faces peeking at her from behind the sofa.

'Yes, little rascals. They're looking forward to being your attendants. I just hope they'll behave. Particularly as we weren't here in time for the rehearsal. Come, children,' she said, turning and pulling them out, giggling, from their hiding spot. 'Come and meet your new aunt.'

Gabriella's face lit up. Like most Brazilians, she adored children. Crouching, she beckoned to the lovely little girl and boy. 'Hello.' She reached out her hands to them. 'Oh, you're so beautiful,' she exclaimed, stroking the little girl's golden curls and smiling at the little boy, who grinned back shyly. They were already dressed, the girl in a pale blue satin bridesmaid's dress that was a tiny replica of her own, and the boy in a page outfit with velvet knee britches and a lace ruffled shirt.

'Ricky is three, and named after you know who.' Constanza rolled her eyes. 'And this is Anita, who's four.'

'What lovely names. Are you really going to help me at my wedding?' Gabriella asked them in a conspiratorial tone. Both children nodded seriously. 'I'm counting on you,' she said, straightening, and took their hands.

At that moment the Contessa hurried in, suitably attired in a rustling blue silk dress and coat. Several rows of large pearls hung about her neck and her ears gleamed with diamonds of the first water. She was followed closely by Sara. 'Ah, Constanza, there you are. I was worried your plane might be held up due to that storm in Germany. I see all is arranged. Now, Gabriella,' she said, turning towards her, 'run downstairs, my love. Ricardo wishes to see you.'

'But it's bad luck for the bridegroom to see the bride on their wedding day before the ceremony,' Constanza exclaimed, sitting up abruptly on the couch. 'He must know that.'

'Rubbish,' her aunt dismissed with a wave of her bejewelled hand.

'If it was me I wouldn't go,' Constanza said, jumping up and straightening the folds of the wedding gown.

'Oh, who cares? It really doesn't matter,' Gabriella muttered.

'At least take the gown off and slip something else on,' Constanza urged.

Their eyes met and, despite her desire to remain cool and aloof, Gabriella nodded.

Slipping into the walk-in-closet, she carefully removed the gown and hung it on a hanger, where its train spread out across the thick-piled beige carpet. She swallowed and her eyes filled with tears. At any other time it would have been the gown of her dreams. She turned quickly away and slipped on a pair of sweats and a short T-shirt that revealed her midriff. Serves him right. She sniffed, raising her chin belligerently and making her way down the wide, ornate corridor painted with frescoes and gold leaf. Tough luck if he didn't approve of her. She was damned if she was going to be everything he wanted.

He'd soon learn.

*   *   *

A knock on the double-panelled gilt door made Ricardo start. He'd been daydreaming for a moment.

'Come in.' He turned and faced the door, which a liveried servant was opening.

'You requested my presence?' Gabriella said with mock sweetness, thrusting her thumbs into the top of her sweats and standing at an angle, her foot drumming the floor.

Ricardo watched her, half-amused, half-irritated. She certainly did not look like a blushing bride preparing for her wedding, which was to take place within hours. He was about to make a pithy comment about her T-shirt when he realised with a touch of humour that she had done it on purpose, to provoke him. He smiled inwardly. Let the wedding take place. Then he would make very sure she never went around looking like this any more. As his wife it would be utterly inappropriate.

'I asked you to come down because I wanted to give you something.' He turned towards the desk and picked up a flat red leather jewel case, which he opened. On a white satin bed lay a splendid diamond necklace and earrings. 'This necklace has been worn by the brides in my family for several generations,' he said, moving towards her. 'It is appropriate that you should wear it too.' He lifted the necklace and laid the box down on a nearby table. 'If you turn around I'll put it on for you.'

She hesitated. He looked so devastatingly handsome. She hadn't expected him to be attired in dark dress uniform with gold braid and buttons, a sword hanging at his side. He looked rather like a prince out of a fairy tale. And it made him seem more remote and unreal.

Should she accept his gift or reject it?

But before she could react he came up behind her and slipped the necklace around her neck. She felt the cool of the white gold and the touch of his fingers on her skin, and a shiver coursed through her as he closed the clasp. Her eyes closed and she let out a sigh. Then his fingers touched her hair. She could feel the warmth of his breath on her neck and stood perfectly still as his fingers trailed down her back and she felt him drop a kiss on the back of her neck.

'There.' He drew back reluctantly. 'Turn around and let me see how you look.'

She turned about obediently, wishing she could find something snappy and intelligent to say, something to set her back on track. But the touch of his fingers and the kiss had been profoundly disturbing.

'Very nice,' he said approvingly, giving her a critical look. 'Or it will be once you are appropriately dressed. You will do very nicely, Princess Gabriella. You are aware that you will be assuming the title from the moment we are married? In other words, in about an hour and a half,' he said, glancing at the flat gold watch on his wrist. 'Try to be on time, okay? Now, where is Constanza?' he said, turning away with a frown. 'I need a quick word with her.'

If looks could kill Gabriella's would have meant his instant demise.

'I believe she's still upstairs,' she muttered through gritted teeth, wishing she had the guts to tear the necklace off and throw it at him. But dignity saved her.

Instead, her eyes flashed in green anger and she spun about without a word. So he thought he could treat her like another of his servants, did he? Well, he had another think coming. She whirled back up the stairs, leaving Ricardo with a pensive look on his face.

He didn't seem to be getting very far with Gabriella.

He hoped that he wasn't making a very grave mistake.

For both of them.

CHAPTER FOUR

As the royal yacht sailed out of Maldoravia's harbour and into the sunset, Prince Ricardo and his bride, the beautiful Princess Gabriella, waved from the deck in a charming manner.

So went the report in the *Maldoravian Gazette*, the Principality's leading newspaper. What the local and international journalists were not aware of was that the newly married couple were barely on speaking terms.

The yacht had sailed to the Italian coast, from where a helicopter had taken them to the nearest airport. From there an official plane had flown them to Ricardo's private Caribbean island next to the Dominican Republic, where they would remain for their honeymoon.

The wedding with all its pomp, the crowds that had waved in the streets as they'd driven from the Cathedral back to the Palace, their journey and their arrival on the island all seemed like a distant dream to Gabriella—as though she'd been an automaton and it had happened to someone else.

Now they were being guided by Ricardo's personal assistant, Baron Alfredo—an elderly white-haired man who had served his father—up to the huge master suite. Gabriella drew in her breath when Alfredo

opened the double doors of a huge room and she saw
the king-size bed. It had not occurred to her that they
would be sleeping in the same room.

What an idiot she was, she chided herself as they
stepped inside. Of course they would be expected to
sleep together. The whole world believed that they
were living a whirlwind romance. She opened her
mouth to protest, but then, seeing the Baron's benign
smile, closed it once more. She would have to wait
until he'd left them alone.

As soon as the door closed behind him Gabriella
moved towards the huge panoramic window overlooking the sea and took a deep breath.

'Ricardo, we shall have to come to some kind of
arrangement,' she said, turning and facing him, head
high, unaware of how lovely she looked framed
against the backdrop of the sea and sky.

'What do you mean?' he asked, taking off his jacket
and depositing it on the back of a rattan armchair.

'Well, this…' Gabriella gestured with her hand
about the room. 'You don't really expect me to sleep
in the same bed, let alone the same room as you?' she
said hotly.

'Naturally we must share a room and a bed,' he
replied in a casual tone, eyeing her calmly. 'Like it or
not, Gabriella, you are now my wife. It would look
very odd if we were to sleep in separate bedrooms.
Particularly on our honeymoon,' he added dryly, his
eyes encompassing her as he spoke. 'I think an international scandal is better avoided, don't you? I have
no desire to be fodder for every tabloid on the planet.'

Gabriella was about to retort that she didn't give a

damn about tabloids, or anyone else for that matter, when the truth of his words sank in. She sat down abruptly on an ottoman and stared out of the window at the coconut trees. She felt a sudden pang of nostalgia, for the scene reminded her very much of home.

'Ricardo, we *have* to come up with something,' she said at last, trying to sound reasonable and grown-up. 'It—it would be impossible to sleep here together. I mean...' She looked away, waved her hand again in a vague gesture, embarrassed for one of the few times in her life.

Ricardo watched her, eyes narrowed, assessing the situation. 'Are you worried about sharing a bed with me, Gabriella?' he asked softly.

'No—yes. Oh, I don't know,' she exclaimed, irritated, rising but still staring out of the window, her back to him.

He stood for a moment watching the line of her tense body, her beautiful figure outlined under a soft linen dress which fitted her to perfection. All at once he recalled her lithe young form gliding through the dark waters of the Brazilian lake, and he moved behind her, slipping his arms around her waist. 'You know, we could deal much better than we have up until now, *cara mia*,' he murmured. 'Why not recognise that we are stuck with one another and make the best of it?'

'That is hardly a romantic statement,' she said pithily, her shoulders stiff. But Ricardo's hands reached up and he massaged them.

'True. But then we are not a very romantic couple, are we?'

'That's the understatement of the year,' she muttered, trying to hold out against the delicious ripples coursing through her as his hands caressed her.

'Nevertheless, it's reality,' he replied, his hands moving lower. 'Of course, that is not to say that we cannot become an extremely romantic couple. It's up to you, *cara*.'

'Oh, you don't understand,' she said, pulling away. 'How could you? After all, this is just an obligation you're fulfilling, and taking me to your bed is merely a part of it.' She drew back and swallowed the tears that surged in her throat. 'I'm going to swim. I need the exercise.'

'Very well,' he said, watching her closely. For a moment he considered taking her in his arms and forcing her to submit, then thought better of it. Better to let her simmer down. 'I shall see you at dinner.' With that he turned on his heel and walked out.

The ocean was deliciously warm and reminded her of Brazil. Gabriella let the water run over her and for a few moments forgot the circumstances of her marriage, giving way to the physical enjoyment of sea, sun and sand.

From the terrace overlooking the beach Ricardo watched her thoughtfully, wondering exactly how he was going to manage his marriage. The sight of her once more in a tiny bikini in the surf sent another rush of desire through him. What would tonight bring? he wondered. With a smile he turned back into the spacious living room. She was his wife. What was it the papers were calling her? 'The most beautiful princess in Christendom'? Well, so she was. What was comical was that he, Europe's most courted bachelor, was married to a woman who right now didn't want to give him the time of day, let alone share a bed with him.

A confident smile broke on his lips as he watched her. Give it some time. Wasn't that what Aunt Elizabetta had counselled? He'd never imagined he'd be taking advice about the conquest of a woman from his elderly aunt, but maybe she was right: give Gabriella some time to get used to her new way of life and the rest would fall into place naturally.

He watched her another few minutes, enjoying the scene, aware of the pulsating desire he was experiencing for her. He *would* give her a little time, but not too long. He wanted her and he would have her. With another confident smile he turned back into the living room, then made his way to the study to make the phone calls that, even on his honeymoon, he could not escape.

Dinner was served on the terrace under the stars. In any other circumstances it would have been the most romantic of settings. But the bride sat in an exquisite green silk designer dress, picking vaguely at the delicious food prepared with great care by the cook and her team, and the conversation was stilted. But the champagne was chilled. Gabriella took a long gulp, ignoring the fact that she very rarely drank alcohol.

Ricardo sat looking coolly sophisticated. At the end of the meal he nursed a brandy as if he had the whole night before him. Nervous, despite her determination to keep up as good a front as him, Gabriella accepted more champagne, twirled her flute and gazed out into the starlit night.

At this rate she would fall asleep, he mused. During the past few weeks he'd only seen her drink lemonade or water. He doubted she'd ever consumed this amount of champagne before. For a moment he thought of telling her to stop, but then decided to leave well alone. The worst that could happen was that she would have a bad head tomorrow morning.

But as the champagne took effect Gabriella's thoughts turned to all that had happened during the past weeks—the changes in her life and the fact that now she had a husband. She peered at him over the rim of her glass, blinking when she saw double.

'Are you feeling okay?' Ricardo said, rising and moving to where she stood leaning precariously on the balustrade, her hair swept back into a silken mass falling down her bronzed back.

'Fine. I'm fine. Just fine,' she mumbled.

'Are you sure?' He turned her around, saw the tears in her eyes and frowned. 'Gabriella, tell me what is wrong, *cara mia*?' His hands slipped to her shoulders.

'Everything,' she hurled at him. 'This is all your fault. If you hadn't insisted we get married none of this would have happened.'

'We're not getting into that all over again, are we?' he said with a sigh. 'It's done now, and we have to live with it.'

'No, we don't. I don't want to live with you,' she cried, a catch in her voice. 'I don't want to be your wife. I don't care what the papers write about us. It doesn't matter. I want out of this marriage. I hate you, and I refuse to be paraded about as your trophy. Like some exotic animal.' Her eyes blazed wet with tears and she downed another gulp of champagne.

'Is that how you think of yourself?' He looked down at her quizzically, a gleam in his eye.

'No,' she spat, 'it's how you think of me.'

'Now that you mention it, there are times when you resemble a tigress,' he commented, still eyeing her with amused if arrogant benevolence.

'How dare you?' she cried, wriggling in his hold. 'It isn't funny. I am not here to amuse you or be treated as your pet dog.'

'Dog? I thought you were a tigress. And tigresses needs to be tamed,' he said, his voice husky with desire as he gripped her shoulders, drawing her firmly towards him. Then before she could move he slipped his arms about her and brought her into him. One hand laced her hair and he drew her head back until her eyes blazed into his. 'The last time I kissed you you didn't dislike it that much, Gabriella. Let's see how you enjoy it this time.' His voice rang low and deep with desire.

Before she could react his lips were closing on hers. Gabriella fought weakly in his arms, but to no avail. Then as his tongue sought hers she experienced a rush of intense heat spiral from her head to the pit of her stomach, and her hands went limp and her breasts throbbed unbearably. Unconsciously she arched, as Ricardo expertly deepened the kiss, and his other hand slid down her back until it reached the delicious curve of her full, rounded bottom. Caressing her, he did what he had done that day at the lake and pressed her closer, forcing her to feel the intensity of his desire.

Every last shred of Gabriella's resistance gave way. She hated Ricardo, detested him, despised everything about him. Yet as their bodies entwined all Gabriella could think of was the scent of him, the raw, unadulterated attraction that overwhelmed her like a spell. She could feel his fingers unzipping her silk dress and knew that she longed to be free of it, to feel him skin to skin. She could barely breathe with the need of him.

'You are beautiful, Gabriella,' Ricardo muttered, slipping the straps of her dress from her shoulders so that it fell to her waist and revealed her small, taut breasts. He gazed down at her perfect body as she threw her head back and leaned against the balustrade. Her eyes closed as his thumb trailed down her throat and he grazed her aching nipples. When he lowered his lips to them she let out a tiny cry of protest and longing.

Ricardo savoured her, revelling in her scent, her skin, in those perfect breasts reacting so innocently yet so intensely to his touch. He knew this was the first time she'd been properly held in a man's arms, knew that although she was full of untamed, unfettered passion, it was up to him to take it slowly, to make it an unforgettable experience whatever happened to them in the future. Her reactions were spontaneous and natural—so much so that he almost laid her on the chaise longue to take her there and then. But sanity intervened and he pulled himself together. It was impossible, he reminded himself through the haze of desire gripping him. Even though she was so full of raw, wild passion, he must hold back.

A noise from inside the living room brought him back to earth with a bang. Hastily he pulled the dress up over her breasts and drew her into his arms, holding her close.

'What is it?' she whispered, opening her eyes.

'Probably just Marco the butler, making sure everything is all right for the night,' he whispered. 'Can you manage?' He smiled down at her now, their eyes meeting in complicity as she struggled to get the straps of her dress back in place and look demure. Then Ricardo turned and stepped back inside the French doors.

Gabriella heard him talking to the butler and dismissing him for the night. She blinked and tried to focus. What had happened to her? How had she allowed him to take her in this fashion? She shook herself and stood erect, her shoulders thrust back, then moved to one of the wrought-iron terrace chairs and sat dizzily down. Her head throbbed and she closed her eyes—only to feel the world spin.

'Oh,' she groaned, dropping it in her hands.

'Are you all right, *cara mia*?' Ricardo moved across the terracotta tiles to where she sat and crouched next to her. 'I think the best place for you is bed—after you've taken a couple of stomach-calming tablets and some water to ensure that you don't feel too bad in the morning.'

Then he swept her into his arms and carried her indoors and up the staircase to the huge bedroom.

Gabriella wanted to struggle, wanted to protest, but felt too dizzy. She must not allow him such liberties, she told herself in the recess of her hazy brain. Somewhere in the back of her mind she felt unhappy, disappointed that this was how she was going to spend her wedding night. But even in her woozy state it occurred to her that if she allowed the marriage to be consummated then she would be caught for ever. The only way she could insist on an annulment was if she didn't allow him to make love to her.

But all these were fleeting wisps of thought that touched the edges of her mind then disappeared as he lay her down among the pillows. She was too weak to protest when he began undressing her, too sleepy to...

Once he'd changed Gabriella into a pair of his pyjamas and tucked her safely into bed, Ricardo looked down at her sleeping form and smiled. Poor Gabriella. She had been through a lot. Silently he undressed himself and, after brushing his teeth, got into bed next to her. Turning off the light, he heard the soft pattern of her breathing next to him and sighed.

This was not going to be easy, he realised, turning on his side. Better try and get some rest. Tomorrow was another day, and he would take it as it came. But it was hard to sleep knowing that she lay curled next to him. Hard not to take her into his arms and make love to this woman who was legally his.

The next morning Ricardo was awoken by a discreet knock on the bedroom door. Glancing at Gabriella's sleeping figure, he rose quietly and slipped into the anteroom.

'Yes, Alfredo, what is it?'

'There was an explosion in the marketplace of Maldoravia fifteen minutes ago, Your Highness. They still don't know if it was a bomb planted by a terrorist group or simply an accident caused by a faulty electrical system in one of the surrounding buildings. As you know, some are very old and the wiring is unsafe. Anyway, Your Highness, it will require your immediate presence back in Maldoravia.'

'Of course. I'll leave at once.'

'Will you be travelling alone?'

He hesitated a moment, then took a decision. 'Yes. There is no point in worrying the Princess. I'll go, and return as soon as I can.'

'Very well.' The Baron gave a small bow and Ricardo closed the door.

Back in the room, he showered and dressed quickly. For a moment he glanced down at his sleeping wife, wondering whether he should wake her. But on second thoughts he decided she was better off resting. He would deal with business and return as soon as was possible.

Leaving the darkened room quietly, he closed the door softly behind him and was on his way.

It was past eleven o'clock by the time Gabriella stretched and yawned and realised that she was not in her own bed. She opened her eyes warily. Then all at once the events of the previous evening hurtled in, and she closed her eyes again with a groan. How could she have behaved in that manner? How could she have let him have his way? How...?

Suddenly it dawned on her that she wasn't lying ravished in a heap—rather that she was comfortably ensconced in a large pair of striped pyjamas which, although practical, were certainly not designed for seduction. She sat up among the pillows, crossed her legs and blinked. There was no sign of Ricardo, though from the dent in the pillows and the thrown-back covers it was obvious that he had slept in the same bed. Rising drowsily, she padded across the marble floor and, rubbing her eyes, went to the window. Perhaps he was downstairs. He must be. She felt a niggling feeling of guilt for having misjudged him. He had not taken advantage of her. Somehow the fact that she had automatically imagined he would made her feel ashamed.

For a moment she watched the coconut trees swaying in the warm morning breeze, then, turning on her heel, she walked into the bathroom and into the shower—where she stood for a good fifteen minutes as the cold water jet cleared her head and her brain. This was not turning out to be quite as simple as she'd imagined. She could not just be difficult, make him realise life was going to be hell and get him to agree to an annulment or a divorce. There was more to it than that. More than she had, as yet, put her finger on. But she was determined to get on top of it. She needed to control the situation, have it her way.

And that, right now, was what seemed to be eluding her.

'What do you mean, he left?' she asked, astonished, half an hour later as she walked into the large tropical living room where Baron Alfredo was awaiting her.

'Your Highness, the Prince was obliged to leave on state business early this morning. An explosion occurred in Maldoravia. The cause is undetermined as yet, but His Royal Highness decided to return home at once.'

'Oh.' Gabriella sat down on the couch with a bang. She should be profoundly relieved that Ricardo had been called away, but instead she felt strangely empty.

'His Royal Highness insisted that you rest and enjoy the holiday. He will be in touch later.'

'Thank you,' she replied with a brief smile. She must think—must decide what to do before it was too late. Ricardo was away. This might be her only chance to turn things in her favour. But what could she do? After all, she was stuck on this wretched island. Anything she did, any move she made, would immediately be reported back to Ricardo. Yet it could be her one opportunity to make her escape and seek her liberty.

For a moment she recalled the evening before—the undeniable desire that had raged between her and Ricardo, the indisputable, irrefutable need she'd experienced to be possessed by him. For a moment she closed her eyes and indulged in fantasy. Then she opened them, gave herself a shake and, boosting her resolve, headed onto the terrace for a cup of coffee.

She didn't trust herself with Ricardo. It was as if he held some kind of spell over her when he touched her. And that, she promised herself in the bright light of day, could not be allowed to happen again. She would never be subjected to any man, however much she might be attracted to him. And the truth was that was all it was: attraction. Not the basis for a solid marriage, of that she was certain. He was overbearing and dictatorial and she had no intention of obeying him— even if she had taken vows to that effect, she recalled uneasily.

One fruit salad and two more coffees later, Gabriella felt fortified enough to begin planning. Her head felt considerably better than it had on waking. Now she must think. This island was close to the Dominican Republic and not far from the US. She still had her credit card. From the Dominican Republic it was only a hop, skip and a jump to Miami, from where she could get a plane back to Brazil. The idea grew on her and she sat back, biting her lip, letting it develop. If she returned to Brazil then of course she would persuade her father's lawyer, Andrade, to go ahead with divorce proceedings. After all, she was a Brazilian subject.

It was brilliant.

Gabriella congratulated herself on her insight and set about implementing the scheme.

She began by seeking out Baron Alfredo and telling him she was planning a shopping trip to Miami the next day. She would pretend to Ricardo that she was bored. Frankly, he was probably too taken up with events in Maldoravia to bother about what she was up to anyway. She would simply pacify him and let him think everything was fine. And before he knew it she would have flown the coop.

As it turned out, she was right.

CHAPTER FIVE

GABRIELLA touched down at Miami International at
ten in the morning. As the private jet that Baron
Alfredo had chartered to take her there from the
Dominican Republic landed, she wondered how she
was going to shake off the two bodyguards and the
chauffeur who had been ordered to accompany her.
She glanced at her mobile phone. As soon as she was
in the terminal she would phone the airline and book
a flight to Rio tonight. But between now and then she
would have to find a way of shedding her entourage.

Soon they were moving through the busy airport.
Then she was in the back of a limo, driving down
I-95 towards Miami Beach, satisfied that she'd managed to make a first-class reservation to Rio for that
evening. The rest would just have to fall into place
along the way, she decided optimistically. She was
determined not to worry about it and to be positive.
She always got her own way, didn't she? So why
should that change?

As the car crossed the MacArthur Causeway and
headed towards Ocean Drive, she sighed and, despite
her determination to get away from him, wondered
what Ricardo was doing right now. She quickly
stopped herself from worrying whether he was safe,
telling herself that it was nothing to her if he was or

not. She had no business caring what happened to him, did she?

After a brief look at the stores on Collins Avenue, Gabriella got back in the limo and continued towards Bal Harbour. It was fundamental that she gave the impression to her bodyguards and chauffeur that she wanted to shop until she dropped, so she wandered through the sophisticated shopping mall, in and out of several boutiques, and stopped in two exquisitely expensive designer stores where she bought a couple of handbags, a T-shirt and two pairs of shoes to justify her expedition, before sitting down at one of the outdoor restaurants and ordering some lunch. When the waitress proposed a glass of champagne she cringed inwardly. She would not be drinking champagne any time soon, she vowed, ordering a mineral water.

The offer of champagne reminded her of just how gentlemanly Ricardo had been, and how caring. She blushed at the thought of him removing her clothes and dressing her in his pyjamas. But she banished that thought quickly and focused instead on thinking up creative excuses for staying in town for the night. No way could she let herself be taken back to the island today, for that would put an end to all her schemes.

After some salad and some thinking, Gabriella decided to tell her bodyguards that she was too tired to return to the island that day and would check into the Ritz Carlton in Coconut Grove. She would tell them that they could have the evening off, since she planned to stay in her suite all evening. She just hoped they would all agree to go off duty—which she doubted, since they seemed to be a permanent fixture—in time

for her to slip out, catch a cab and make it to the
airport in time for her Rio flight.

By the time he reached Maldoravia it had already been
established that the cause of the explosion was, as had
been suspected, bad electrical wiring in an ancient
building in the old town. Ricardo was glad that the
cause of the incident was not terrorism, but that did
not alter the dimension of the tragedy: the fact that
seven were dead and three injured was distressing
enough.

He had visited the bereaved families, and the injured
at the hospital, and only now did he have time to think
about his wife. Once he was back at the Palace in his
office he began to pick up his voice messages. After
that he would call her. But the first message on his
machine was from Baron Alfredo, saying that
Gabriella had gone to Miami for the day.

He frowned slightly and replayed it, then shrugged.
Perhaps she was bored, being left on the island by
herself. After all there was not much to do there.
Probably better that she distract herself with shopping.
But when he tried to reach her on her mobile phone
he discovered it was turned off, and he experienced a
stab of disappointment.

When next morning Alfredo rang to say that
Gabriella had remained in Miami for the night and
would be returning to the island later in the day, he
really frowned. A niggling sensation of doubt assailed
him, which he found difficult to shake off. He dragged
his fingers through his thick dark hair and leaned back
in the leather desk chair feeling uneasy, wishing he

could leave at once. But that was impossible. He had been working most of the night, and today he had to attend the funerals. He glanced at his watch. He had no time now to worry about Gabriella, who would be back on the island in a few hours anyway. But something disturbed him.

It was only at the end of the day—once he'd returned exhausted from the burial processions and funerals, and with the press still awaiting his comments—that he received the news that Gabriella was nowhere to be found; her hotel suite was empty and her bags were gone. Somehow he was not surprised.

'Damn her,' he exclaimed, moving away from the crowd of journalists who were waiting to interview him. He glanced at his watch. The first thing he had to do was find out where she'd escaped to. Was she still in the US? Where was he to begin looking for his errant wife? Those incompetent bodyguards. He would have something to say to them.

But, in all fairness, if she had gone to her suite—as they'd assured him she had—and told them she would be staying there for the night, there was no way they could have avoided her escape. He had no doubt that she had found some creative manner of leaving the hotel. After all, he had sent them to protect her, not to spy.

Ricardo experienced a rush of anger. She had probably escaped in some unorthodox fashion. What the hell did she think she was doing? Didn't she realise that the games were over, that she was his wife now? Gabriella was a thorough pest, and right now he could throttle her for making such a nuisance of herself. Not to mention the underlying worry of not knowing where she was and the fear that something might have happened to her for which he would hold himself directly responsible.

It felt good to see the Corcovado, the Sugar Loaf Mountain, and Rio spreading out below her in the early-morning light. As the plane circled the city Gabriella let out a sigh of relief. The plan had worked. She was on her way home—where *she* called the shots. Soon this whole episode with Ricardo would be nothing but a nightmare.

Well, not quite a nightmare, she recognised uncomfortably. There had been wonderful moments—moments she would have difficulty in forgetting. But that was not something she planned to dwell on.

Soon she was outside the air terminal, feeling the familiar blast of damp heat. She had arranged for the hotel where she planned to stay in Rio to send a car to pick her up. Already at the terminal she'd felt good, knowing she was back on her own turf, hearing the reassuring buzz of people talking nineteen to the dozen and the sounds of samba music and laughter. She knew that she had finally come home. But now, instead of the rush of triumph she'd expected, she felt strangely empty, as if a large vacuum had suddenly popped into her life. But she banished that thought.

As soon as she arrived at the Copacabana Palace, Gabriella called Andrade, her father's chief lawyer and executor, and told him to send the jet to pick her up and take her back to the family estate. He promptly fulfilled her request, and a few hours later she was flying over rainforest, huge stretches of farmland and varying countryside as the plane headed north. She had set up a meeting with the lawyer for the following day.

Gabriella still hadn't faced the fact that she would have to talk to Ricardo and explain her actions. Or maybe she wouldn't, she reflected, drinking a cola and curling up in the big leather seat. Maybe she wouldn't explain anything at all. After all, her actions spoke for themselves, didn't they? After this he would probably be happy to be rid of her.

Instead of making her happy, that last thought left her somewhat gloomy. Of course it would be an international scandal, and she hated the thought of subjecting him to that after he'd been really quite decent to her. The idea was rather lowering, and for a moment she felt a wave of sadness. But then she pulled herself together and justified her behaviour. It was just one of those things that couldn't be helped. Collateral damage. That was how she had to think of it. After all, it was he who had been so determined to go ahead with the wedding. So it was basically all his fault.

Still, even though she shrugged and picked up a magazine to read, she found it impossible to concentrate. Somehow Ricardo's image, his deep dark eyes and enigmatic smile, kept interfering.

'Damn him,' she mumbled, throwing the magazine into the seat across the aisle and leaning back, closing her eyes. She had finally rid herself of the man. That was what she'd wanted, surely? Then why instead of elation did she feel deflated? It made absolutely no sense.

No sense at all.

*   *   *

'You *what*?' Mae Isaura, Gabriella's old nanny exclaimed, her hands firmly planted on her wide hips, her girth framed in the doorway of Gabriella's room.

'I told you,' Gabriella muttered, pretending to unpack. 'I left him. I don't want to be married to him, Isaura. I don't want to be married to anyone. It was crazy of Father to force us. It just wasn't fair. To him or me.' She turned, lifted a blouse from her tote bag and glanced at it. 'This needs ironing.'

'Do not try and change the subject, Gabriella.'

'I'm not, I merely said that this blouse—'

'Oh, I wish you were small again. I tell you, if you were, you would have a very sore bottom by now, you naughty child. You have no business to behave in this manner. You will stop unpacking and return to your husband at once.'

'No, I won't,' Gabriella threw back. 'I refuse.' The two women confronted one another, eyes blazing, as they had so often over the years: Isaura, small and wide and dark, the only person to whom the girl had ever been known to give way; Gabriella, tall, beautiful and autocratic, her green eyes alive with determined zeal. 'I refuse to live with him, Isaura, to go back to that silly Principality with all its formal ways and protocol and stuffiness. Why, he barely talked to me when we were there. It's stifling, unbearable. I won't.' She whirled around to face the window with her arms crossed protectively over her breasts

'Gabriella, you are too old for tantrums. You are a married woman now, not a child. I'm actually surprised this man has allowed you to get away with this. He seemed a sensible sort to me. And very much a man. He won't take kindly to what you've done. You have humiliated him in front of the world. You should be ashamed of yourself.'

'He asked for it,' she mumbled, knowing she would have a hard time defending this position.

'Well, this time *you've* asked for it, *minha querida*,' Isaura said pithily. 'And I shall have no sympathy for you when you reap the results of this mischief. You'll deserve anything that comes to you.' With that dire warning she turned on her heel and closed the door smartly behind her, leaving Gabriella to brood on her own.

'What do you mean, she's gone?' The Contessa sat ramrod-straight in the high, tapestried Queen Anne chair, shocked, sending a horrified glance to Sara, who stood close by.

'Exactly what I said, Aunt,' Ricardo said, flinging himself down on the brocade sofa opposite. 'She simply upped and left—disappeared. She pretended she was going shopping in Miami, took a suite for the night in a hotel, told the staff she was staying in for the evening, then packed her bags and—away.' He snapped his fingers expressively.

'But where has she gone?' Sara asked, her expression worried.

'I'm not certain,' he replied, eyes narrowing, 'but I have a fairly good hunch that she's gone home to Brazil. After all, where else would she go? London?

Paris? She had some notion that she wanted to be a model. But I don't think she would risk exposing herself right now, when all the press will be at her heels.'

'Poor child,' the Contessa murmured, shaking her coiffed silver head. 'I think both of you have been placed in a most awkward situation.'

'Well, I didn't expect you to react like that,' Ricardo said haughtily. 'I just want to try and avoid an international scandal.' He passed a hand through his hair and sighed. 'She's been nothing but trouble from the moment I accepted Gonzalo's invitation.'

'Is that all that worries you, Ricardo?'

'Well, no. Of course I'm worried about her whereabouts. But I'll not let her make a fool out of me.' He nodded to Sara, who indicated discreetly that she would leave the two of them alone.

The Contessa raised her brows. Always that wretched Maldoravian pride, she reflected with an inner sigh. It might not, she reflected ruefully, do Ricardo any harm to be made to realise he was not the only fish in the sea. 'Well, I suppose if she's gone home that makes it much easier,' she said blandly. 'After all, if she's nothing but a nuisance to you, then you are well rid of her.'

'What?' He looked across at her, amazed.

'You just said that she has been nothing but trouble from day one,' the Contessa reasoned.

'That's all very well,' he muttered, rising and pacing the room. 'But she's my wife, and I'm damned if I'll have her leaving me in the middle of our honeymoon, making a fool of me to the world. How do you think that will look to the press?' he demanded.

'Ah, I see.' The Contessa raised her brows slightly. 'Appearances.'

'Yes, Aunt, appearances,' Ricardo muttered through gritted teeth. 'These are things that will have to be considered and carefully administered.'

'Mmm. I suppose you're right,' she replied, eyeing him with a touch of humour. 'But, you know, I really wonder if perhaps Gabriella isn't right, and if you should bring this marriage to an end despite the scandal.'

'What did you say?' Ricardo rose and stared at her, astonished. 'Of all people, I never thought I'd hear *you* express such a view, Aunt. Frankly, I am shocked to hear you say it.'

'I'm simply being reasonable. After all, there is no love lost between you, and it will be nothing but a seven-day wonder that's fast replaced by some other, juicier scandal.'

'Rubbish. I won't hear of it.'

'So you plan to go after her?'

'Of course I plan to go after her,' he answered in a withering tone. 'Despite this crazy notion of yours, she's still my wife, and she will be brought back here where she belongs and made to behave as befits her position.'

'I see. Well, it's entirely up to you.' The Contessa shrugged lightly, picked up her embroidery and remained annoyingly calm.

'I shall travel to Brazil and take any decisions there. At least we will be seen to be together. Perhaps we should not have allowed ourselves to be held hostage to Gonzalo's deathbed wishes,' he added thoughtfully.

'Still, there was little to be done. His will meant she would have lost all her money had I not insisted we go through with the ceremony.' He shook his head as his personal secretary appeared in the doorway.

'Your Royal Highness is expected,' the secretary said with a small bow.

'Of course.' With an automatic smile Ricardo said goodbye to his aunt and left the salon.

'I'm afraid what you ask is impossible,' Andrade, the white-haired lawyer, replied to Gabriella's request to begin divorce proceedings.

'But why?' she asked, spinning around and facing him full on.

'Because, *querida*, from the moment you married the Prince you became a Maldoravian citizen. You are now subject to the laws of the Principality,' he said, flipping through some papers. 'I took the liberty of doing some research on the subject before you married. Just out of general interest, you understand. For any court to grant you a divorce in Maldoravia, you would have to first prove that you have lived together for at least six months,' he said, checking the items with his index finger, 'secondly prove that the marriage has failed after a sufficient period of life in common to have given it a fair trial, and then have a period of separation in which you agree to counselling and are open to reconciliation. If after all that, and a two-year period of separation, both of you still feel that there are irreconcilable differences that cannot be surmounted, then the case can be heard in court. Even then it is not certain that a divorce will be granted.

The Constitution of Maldoravia is very ancient and old-fashioned, and its laws on the matter of divorce are very strict.'

'You're joking?' Gabriella sat down opposite him, deflated. 'But that's simply awful—what am I to do?' She threw up her hands in despair. 'I can't be stuck with him for the rest of my life. It's not fair.' Perhaps an annulment was the answer...

At that moment a servant appeared. 'Dona Gabriella, a visitor has arrived.'

'A visitor?' She looked up sharply.

'Yes, *senhora*. Your husband, the Prince, awaits you.'

'Goodness.' Gabriella paled. 'How has he got here so quickly?' She braced herself, tried to feel very brave and very grown-up. This was it. 'Please wait a moment, Andrade, while I receive my—the Prince.' Tossing her dark hair back, she marched through the door and prayed for the right words to be sent to her.

As he had on his first visit to the Guimaraes mansion, Ricardo heard the sound of fine heels on marble. He stiffened, turned towards the window and stood erect, hands clasped behind his back, staring out at the tropical landscape. When he heard her enter he waited a moment before turning around. When he did he caught his breath. She was perfectly lovely, her colour heightened, her eyes bright, her breasts heaving with anxiety. How he wished he could take two strides across the room and take her in his arms, teach her how to love and be loved. Instead he kept a cool, indifferent expression on his face and cleared his throat.

'Hello, Gabriella,' he said, as coldly as he could. The rush of desire was impossible to ignore.

'Hello, Ricardo.' She hesitated before advancing into the room, the silence broken only by the sound of the waves rolling in the distance. Their eyes met, held. Then she looked away and sat down, indicating the white sofa opposite her.

'I think we need to have a talk,' he said at last, remaining standing.

'What is there to talk about?' she asked, pretending to straighten her skirt. The shock of seeing him again was far greater than she'd expected. All at once scenes from the terrace on their Caribbean honeymoon island surfaced, and she swallowed. Why did he affect her in this way?

'Gabriella, we need to talk about the future. I cannot live with a wife who feels she is obliged to flee from me the minute my back is turned.'

'Then let's get divorced and be done with it.'

'Yes, let's.' He nodded. 'I think you're right. That is probably the best solution.'

She looked up, her eyes awash with amazement. 'But—you'd agree to a divorce?'

'If it is the only solution—why, yes. I certainly don't want to live with you under the present circumstances. It would make life impossible. And I really don't have time to come after you every time you run away or play the fool with this capricious behaviour.'

Gabriella's jaw dropped. She'd imagined everything: outrage, anger, anything but indifference. She clenched her fists. 'Well, good,' she muttered through gritted teeth. 'How convenient that my lawyer is already here.'

'Is he? That's great. Then why don't we get on with it?' Ricardo smiled politely. 'Just call him in and we can settle matters immediately. I would quite like to get out of here before dusk.' He glanced at the sky, then at his watch. 'It will get dark pretty soon now, I should think.'

Without a word, her lips tightly closed, Gabriella rose and rang the bell. A servant appeared immediately. 'Tell Dr Andrade to join us, please,' Gabriella said, her head in turmoil. This was not at all how things were meant to pan out. Not that she had any clear idea of what the correct script should be—simply that this wasn't it.

Andrade entered the room, all smiles.

'Your Highness—how nice to see you again so soon after your wedding.'

Ricardo smiled and shook hands with the man.

Gabriella's mind was working frantically.

'I hope you had a good trip?' the lawyer continued, accepting the chair being offered to him.

'Not as good as it could be, under the present circumstances,' Ricardo countered with a grave look. 'I believe you are already aware,' he said, with a brief mocking glance at Gabriella, 'that my wife and I find we do not suit and would like an immediate divorce?'

'Yes, that's right,' Gabriella agreed nervously, trying to pretend to herself that the words 'my wife' did not affect her in any shape or form. 'As I told you we—we want to get divorced. We—' She looked up and caught Ricardo's eyes.

'But that is impossible,' the lawyer repeated, shaking his head. 'Your Royal Highness, I just told Gabriella, before you arrived… Let me explain. Since you were not married in Brazil, the courts here have no jurisdiction over your marriage. Any divorce would have to follow Maldoravian law. As I mentioned to Gabriella, a minimum of six months in cohabitation followed by two years' physical separation would be necessary for you to even contemplate such an action. Plus, you would have to go through a reconciliation process and all manner of things. I'm afraid I really can't help you immediately.'

'I see.' Ricardo's expression gave little away.

'But that's so unfair,' Gabriella exclaimed once again. 'Ricardo, you're the Prince—surely you could change the law if you wanted to?'

'Changing the law at a whim is not within my rights,' he remarked dryly.

'Well, I'm sure you could do *something*. After all, it's clear that we can't do it that way. Isn't it?' Her voice was pleading now.

'It appears we have little choice, *cara*.'

'But that's ridiculous.'

'Maybe,' he said, eyeing her steadily, 'but by the look of it we will have to make the best of it.'

'Oh!' Gabriella got up, clenching her fists as she was prone to do in moments of utter frustration. 'Are you saying that I must return with you to that—that stuffy, mouldy, unbearable place, and wither away there for *six months*?'

'That, madam, would appear to be the case,' Ricardo said with a small nod of affirmation.

'But I'm a Brazilian. I'm not Maldo—whatever it is,' she cried, beseeching Andrade for help.

'From the moment you married you became a Maldoravian citizen, and you are now subject to that country's law,' Andrade replied apologetically. 'And by that law your husband can command you to return and live by his side, whether you like it or not. As I told you before, it is a principality that still holds on to old, time-worn traditions. Particularly where marriage is concerned.'

'Oh, I don't believe it,' Gabriella exclaimed, turning and peering at Ricardo through narrowed eyes. 'You knew all this,' she threw accusingly. 'You knew we couldn't get divorced quickly.'

'Actually, I wasn't aware of all the difficulties, having never contemplated the possibility,' Ricardo said calmly. 'But I think Dr Andrade is right. If we wish to proceed in this matter we shall have to follow Maldoravian law and take legal counsel there. In which case the sooner we get back there and get on with it the better—don't you agree?' He glanced once more at his watch. 'Could you be ready, say, in half an hour?'

'It's preposterous,' an exhausted Gabriella repeated to the patient Contessa, who was doing her embroidery while lending a sympathetic ear. 'Why can't we just get divorced and be done with it? After all, it's not as if either of us wants to stay married.' Gabriella whirled around to seek the older woman's agreement.

'Mmm. Of course, one must take into account that the customs here are not as modern as in other parts of the world,' the Contessa countered tactfully, snipping a thread. 'I think the general consensus is that people should try and give their marriage a chance before taking a decision to end it.' She glanced up, caught Gabriella's brooding expression and smothered a smile.

But she was worried about the two young people. It was obvious to anyone that a deep attraction lay between them. You only had to be in the same room to pick up the tense vibes that surrounded the couple. But she was too much of a diplomat to point this out to her errant new niece and her proud, aristocratic nephew. Unfortunately they were going to have to find things out for themselves, she thought with a sigh.

And, to make things worse, Ambrosia, Ricardo's ex-mistress, had arrived on the island that morning. Or so she'd heard from Constanza, who was here for the weekend. The bush telegraph in the Principality functioned at great speed. What could that young woman be up to? she wondered. Surely she would have lost interest in Ricardo now that he was married to another and there was no possibility of her becoming Princess.

Or would she?

The Contessa mused over the matter for several moments while Gabriella sulked by the window. Ambrosia was ambitious, ruthless, and a man-eater. Perhaps she planned to remain in Ricardo's life anyway? The Contessa had never understood what had drawn those two together in the first place. Sex, she supposed, was the answer.

Again the Contessa glanced at Gabriella: so young, so beautiful, so used to getting her own way, and so bewildered by a whole new set of circumstances. The Contessa was quite surprised that Ricardo, known for his prowess with women, had not managed better in this quarter.

'Have you seen Ricardo this morning?' she asked casually, rethreading her needle with a different-coloured silk.

'No, I haven't. He gets up before I get up and goes to sleep after I'm asleep,' Gabriella announced, unaware of how huffy she sounded and of how much that statement proclaimed.

'I see. Well, he must be very busy.'

'I suppose so. Aunt Elizabetta, what am I going to do?' Gabriella sat down on the velvet ottoman near the Contessa and turned her big flashing green eyes towards the older woman. 'I mean, we can't go on living like this,' she cried despairingly, waving her hands. 'It's perfectly ridiculous, don't you think?'

'Yes, I do. I think both of you should grow up and face your responsibilities,' the Contessa remarked calmly.

'What do you mean?' Gabriella sat up straighter, surprised at the response. She'd been looking for sympathy, not a lecture.

'Well, to put it in a nutshell, like it or not you're married—and will remain so for at least two and a half years. If it was me I would make the best of it. Right now you and Ricardo seem to spend the better part of your time avoiding one another. That is not much of a life for either you or him.'

'But what can I possibly do?'

'How about seducing him?'

'Sedu—' Gabriella stared at her, aghast. 'Aunt Elizabetta!' she exclaimed. 'I'm shocked.'

'Why? I wasn't always the age I am now, you know. I can very well remember what it was like to be attracted to a very seductive and handsome man.'

Gabriella jumped off the stool. She was wearing a pretty patterned peasant skirt and a blouse tied at her waist. With her long dark hair and flashing eyes she looked a little like a beautiful gipsy.

'How can I seduce a man that—well, a man who doesn't want me?' she blurted out woefully.

'Doesn't want you?' The Contessa frowned. 'Are you sure? I'm surprised to hear that. I had the impression—' She cut herself off, realising she was about to say too much. 'Well, of course you must know. After all, you are his wife.'

'Much good that does me,' Gabriella muttered. 'Why, after what happened on our honeymoon, he's never even— What I mean to say is, we sleep in the same bed and... Oh, this is too embarrassing—too ridiculous,' she exclaimed, letting out a deep breath.

'You mean to tell me that you are still a virgin?' the Contessa asked quietly.

A flush extended up Gabriella's long slim throat. 'I...yes.'

'Hmm.'

'Aunt, that is not helpful,' Gabriella cried in frustration. 'I don't know what to do.'

'I already told you what to do,' the Contessa said philosophically, a smile hovering about her lips. 'I'm sure that he'll at least be surprised.'

CHAPTER SIX

'RICARDO, darling.'

The husky voice reached him from across the terrace of the Royal Yacht Club and there was no mistaking its origin. Ambrosia stood tall and elegant, her long tanned legs showing below her short tennis skirt, her sleek blonde hair falling on her trim shoulders. She swung her racket casually as she approached. 'It's been an age, darling. I hear that you married?' She looked straight into Ricardo's eyes, a flash of anger quickly concealed as she smiled generously, then let her tongue flick her lips before reaching up to kiss him lightly on both cheeks.

Ricardo caught a whiff of her familiar perfume and experienced a moment's regret. He'd had good times with Ambrosia, even if she was a handful and could never have become his wife. He allowed his hand to slip to her waist. 'You look wonderful, Ambrosia. Tennis obviously suits you. A new lover, perhaps?' he murmured in a lower voice, aware that half the club was watching them.

'Oh, Ricky. We aren't all as faithless as you,' she said with a pout. 'Did you think I would bounce back that quickly?' She leaned back and looked up into his eyes.

'You've never lacked for male company.'

'And I could say the same to you about women,'

she snapped. 'As soon as my back was turned you went off and married. A nineteen-year-old virgin, I hear. How charming. How very quaint. You must be enjoying teaching her all your tricks.'

'Ambrosia, you sound positively jealous,' Ricardo remarked smoothly.

'What if I am?' She raised a suggestive brow and raised her mouth to his ear. 'If you get bored teaching your novice, you can always give me a call.'

'Well, they say that jealousy can provide a lot of spice,' he murmured, 'but we must remember that I'm a married man now.' He was breathing in her scent, seeing the sexy curve of her breast and taking note of the obvious offer she was making.

'I'm not difficult,' she responded in a low, husky voice that left him in no doubt as to her intentions. 'We're sophisticated people, Ricky, darling. What has marriage got to do with us? I like you in bed. You like me. Do your duty to your little brood mare; get her pregnant and get yourself an heir. I presume that this is what all this is about, right? Then we can get on with having fun.'

Ricardo looked down at her for a brief moment. Then he tweaked her cheek and laughed. 'You are always full of surprises, Ambrosia. A man could never become bored with you.'

'Perhaps you should have remembered that sooner,' she responded waspishly. Then, with a smile, she turned and raised her hand to her mouth. 'Oh, my goodness, isn't that your wife over there? She really does have a spectacular figure. Funny. She still looks awfully…untouched, if you know what I mean. I've heard half the men here at the club are taking bets.'

'Bets on what?' he frowned glancing in Gabriella's direction.

'Oh, nothing, really. There's just this rumour going about that says she's still a virgin. The odds on it are pretty high. I must say, it would be funny if she was. Though unlikely, I imagine?' Ambrosia raised her finely pencilled brows once more, then moved away before he could answer.

Ricardo watched as Gabriella and his sister Constanza entered the club, accompanied by Constanza's husband, the handsome blond Count Wilhelm of Wiesthun, and their children, to whom Gabriella seemed to have taken. He watched as she kneeled down in the most natural fashion to tie his niece's trainer lace, which had come undone. Then she raised her head and their eyes met across the large terrace, past the white wicker furniture with the blue and white striped cushions, past the tropical plants and the waiters weaving in and out among the tables with trays of cocktails.

So the whole club was betting on whether he'd bedded his wife or not? Well, damn them! He would not be made a public fool. So much for all the gentlemanliness he'd shown towards Gabriella. Now he was determined to make love to her—whatever the consequences!

Who was the woman Ricardo had been smiling at in such an intimate fashion? Gabriella sensed her pulse race and a rush of heat grip her. She'd never felt anything like this before. But seeing him so close, so intimate with another woman, had left her seething. She might not want him herself, she thought, taking little Anita's hand and leading her to their table, her head high, but she wouldn't be humiliated in front of the whole Principality. So that was why Ricardo hadn't tried to sleep with her again—hadn't attempted to make love to her. He had a mistress.

At the first opportunity, she leaned across to Constanza. 'Who is that woman over there?' she asked, pointing discreetly to the table where Ambrosia sat holding court, laughing expansively, throwing her head back and crossing her long slim legs provocatively.

'That? Oh, that's no one important,' Constanza lied, fussing over her daughter. 'Now where on earth is Nanny? Gabriella, have you seen her?'

'She was taking little Ricky to the loo. But, please, Constanza,' Gabriella insisted, 'don't pretend you don't know. Tell me who she is.'

'Who?' Constanza still acted as if she didn't understand.

'That blonde woman Ricardo was talking to so intimately only moments ago. I got the impression that perhaps—' Gabriella cut off, twisting her hands agitatedly in her lap, unable to continue. It was ridiculous to be nervous. Why should she care what he did? She wanted a divorce, didn't she? So what was she worried about? Who cared what Ricardo got up to?

Constanza glanced up, relieved at the sight of Ricardo crossing the club restaurant towards them.

'Ah, here he is. You can ask him yourself,' she said quickly.

'Hello,' he said standing next to the table. 'May I join you?'

'Why, of course! Ricky, darling!' Constanza exclaimed. 'Sit down here, next to your wife.' She smiled brightly as Ricardo allowed the waiter to draw up a chair. Then he sat down next to Gabriella and slipped his hand casually over hers.

'Everything okay, *cara*? You look a little pale.'

'I'm fine.' She swallowed and tried to ignore the electric shock that pulsated through her the minute his skin touched hers.

'I certainly hope so.' His thumb began to caress the inside of her palm and Gabriella had to muster every inch of self-control not to let out a ragged sigh. She breathed thankfully when the waiter appeared with shrimp cocktails and he was obliged to let her go. Why, oh, why did he have this effect on her? Surely it was madness?

But instead of remaining coolly aloof, as he normally did, the next thing Gabriella felt was Ricardo's hand gently caressing the inside of her thigh. She drew in her breath and sent a furious glance in his direction—to which he paid little attention. There was no room to move, no option but to pretend she wasn't dying of desire. When his fingers reached further, only masterly self-control made it possible for her to continue to maintain her poise, which was evaporating fast. How could he do this? How dared he? What right did he have to ignore her one minute, then seduce her almost publicly the next? It was outrageous, and she would have something to say to him once they were alone.

Only when he knew that she was thoroughly aroused did Ricardo remove his hand and continue with his lunch, content in the knowledge that although his wife might pretend to dislike him, her dislike did not extend to her sexual attraction for him. But enough for now. He had given her a taste of what was to come. Let her simmer for a while.

At least until tonight.

The state dinner with foreign dignitaries had taken longer than expected. Gabriella was glad to kick off her high heels and throw herself onto the bed.

During the meal she'd been seated next to a Portuguese minister who spoke no English. It was fast becoming clear that her knowledge of languages and her ease and gifts as a hostess were considered a great bonus by the government of Maldoravia, which made every use of her it could. She was spared no dinner or luncheon where it was thought that she could be an asset. And, to her surprise, Gabriella found that she had a talent for diplomacy and entertaining. Even the Prime Minister had hinted to her that she might like to broach certain subjects to her neighbour and see what answers she got.

Despite her desire to find everything she could that was wrong with Maldoravia, Gabriella had to admit that it was rather fun to be given important missions and see if by directing the conversation with apparent insouciance she could pick up on what needed to be known through veiled comments. She also had the advantage of being very young. This misled a lot of people, who believed her questions to be mere curiosity and often revealed far more than they might otherwise have intended. Why, only tonight she'd learned of plans for a new trade agreement Portugal wanted to get into with Maldoravia simply by fluttering her long lashes at the Portuguese minister and hanging on to his every word. She had learned early that men loved being the centre of a woman's attention, and played this card to the full. Tomorrow, first thing, she would tell the Prime Minister, who had a special affection for her.

Letting her head drop back on the armchair's cushions, she closed her eyes. There was no sign of Ricardo, who had become increasingly elusive since that day at the yacht club. In fact that night he had left on a state visit to Denmark and had only returned this morning. They had barely spoken. He seemed so distant and inaccessible, and all her plans to seduce him had come to nothing. She let out a sigh. It really didn't matter any more as he was probably making love to his mistress. And, actually, in view of her plans for the future it was probably better this way. What she must do was begin to map out her life after Ricardo. But that, for some inexplicable reason, seemed a difficult task to undertake. The future remained hazy.

Not that it was far off, she reminded herself severely. The time since their return from Brazil had sped by, and the remaining months of the obligatory six needed to complete the period of cohabitation would fast come to a close. She sighed, fiddled with the fringe of one of the cushions that adorned the bed, and tried to persuade herself that she was happy it was coming to an end. Soon they could separate, even if they couldn't get a divorce. So why did she feel so melancholy every time she glanced at a calendar or caught sight of the date of a newspaper? There really was no explaining it.

Laying her head back, Gabriella gave way to exhaustion. Not physical exhaustion, but something else that she'd never known before. As though all the joy of life had suddenly seeped out of her being and there was nothing left to look forward to any more.

After seeing off the last of his official guests, Ricardo made his way up the wide marble staircase and approached the apartments he shared with his wife. It had been a long day, and an even longer evening. The past few weeks had been fraught, with too much work and too little time to relax, he reflected wearily. And too little time to dedicate to trying to save his increasingly chilly relationship with his wife. Perhaps tomorrow he would simply tell Baron Alfredo that he was taking the day off and take Gabriella out on his yacht. If she would agree to come.

He sighed as he turned the door handle of the apartment, and hesitated a moment. This was not proving to be an easy relationship. Gabriella was polite, but cold. She made it abundantly clear that she wanted as little to do with him as possible. He silently entered the small salon but she was nowhere to be seen. Then, tugging at his bow tie, he moved towards the bedroom and stopped in the doorway at the sight of her lying on the bed, eyes closed, her hair splayed over the velvet cushions. Goodness, she was lovely: so young, so beautiful, so enchanting—not to mention sexy.

Ricardo moved across the room and gazed down at her for a long moment. Then he sat down carefully on the bed and allowed his fingers to trail gently through the thick long mass of her silky hair until he reached the contour of her face.

Gabriella opened her eyes, startled. 'Ricardo,' she exclaimed, trying to sit up.

But he kept his hand to her face, bringing the other one down on the other side of her, forcing her back among the cushions. 'My lovely wife,' he murmured. 'My beautiful, unattainable virgin wife.' Then, before she could do more than let out a tiny cry, his mouth came down on hers—not tenderly or caringly, but with a firm, hard movement of possession.

Her lips parted and against her will she felt his tongue seek hers, felt the charge of molten lava shoot from her breasts to her core. Despite every urge to resist, every part of her brain telling her this was not what she wanted, her breasts ached and her body arched. This couldn't be happening. She mustn't allow it to happen. Yet when she felt Ricardo's arm slip below her waist and he moved over her, his arms bracing on either side of her body, his eyes piercing into hers, there was little she could do—little she wanted to do.

'Ricardo, no. We mustn't—please,' she murmured, making a half-hearted attempt to move. Part of her brain was remembering that what she wanted was a divorce while the other half gave way to the desire for his fingers to caress her once more. What was it about this man that riveted her so? What was it that made it impossible for her to refuse him?

One hand glided over her soft silk dress while the other reached to slide down its side zipper. She should resist, make it quite clear that she had no intention of...

But the next thing she knew she was lying naked before him. How it had happened she didn't quite know, only that he was standing over her now, his hair windswept, still in his tux, his bow tie dangling about his neck, his shirt collar open, his expression completely different from that of the man she'd become used to in the past weeks.

'You're so lovely,' he exclaimed, reaching down and trailing his fingers from her neck, down past the taut tips of her breasts until he reached the soft mound between her thighs, where he stopped, letting his fingers slip deeper.

A sigh escaped her and her eyes closed. She wanted to resist, wanted to play the game—as she was sure people like that woman she'd seen at the yacht club did. But she couldn't, didn't know how, only knew that at this moment she could refuse him nothing.

After several minutes of expert caresses, when he felt that Gabriella was ready and longing for him, Ricardo removed his hand and undressed himself.

Gabriella opened her eyes. Part of her longed for him, longed to become a woman—his woman. The shock of this revelation hit home as she watched him slip out of his tux. This man, whom she had every reason to detest, who treated her with cold indifference, was the one she wanted to love her. It made no sense. That she should feel this torrid, uncontrollable attraction for him held no logic; it went against everything about which she'd convinced herself: that she wanted to be free of him. Yet now she could not stop herself. For the truth was, she knew he would stop immediately if she requested it; he was a gentleman, as she'd discovered that night on the island. But that, she knew, would be impossible for her—she wanted him, wanted him more than anything else in the world right now, however bad she might feel tomorrow morning. After this it would be far more difficult to escape him. Although, to her deep distress, he had shown no signs of wanting to persuade her to stay.

All these thoughts conflicted in her mind as Ricardo lay back down next to her on the bed and took her in his arms. Oh, how she wished that she were less confused, Gabriella cried inwardly. That she knew what she really wanted.

'Gabriella, my Gabriella,' he murmured, in a voice she'd never heard before, which left her heart aching. 'You may not want to be my wife,' he muttered huskily, 'but nevertheless I will teach you what it is to be a woman.' His thumb grazed the tip of her breast while his other hand investigated further.

There was nothing she could do, no resistance she could muster. All reason flew to the wind as his lips came down on her breast, his hands roamed her body and sought her core. She was experiencing love for the first time. Suddenly she felt a deep rising ache within her that she thought would never end, and she arched her body towards Ricardo. Then the spiral gave way, and she shuddered with joy as he brought her to some peak and she experienced her first orgasm.

Ricardo smiled down as she lay limp in his arms, satisfied that, whatever happened after this, he—her husband—had been the first to give her the experience. Then slowly he positioned himself over her and looked down into her eyes. And it was then that he knew he could not let her go. This woman whom he'd been landed with so unexpectedly had, he realised with something of a shock, become part of his life. And now he was about to possess her.

'I'll try not to hurt you,' he whispered, his voice turning gentle as he read the flash of fear in her eyes. This soft and pliant lovely creature was a very different woman from the Gabriella who had faced him every day with icy pride and from whom he had become so distant. This was the vibrant, feeling, sensitive creature whom he had been certain all along existed beneath her façade. Holding her now in his arms, he entered her in one quick movement, heard her tiny gasp of pain, and held her tighter, kissing her lips, her eyes, her hair while he thrust deep within her, unable to hold back from losing himself in her depths. Soon he felt her pain give way to pleasure, felt her body easing into the rhythm of his as naturally as if they had been making love for years. Now they were riding on the crest of a rolling wave, skimming the surf, roaring towards completion. Then, when he could bear it no longer, he felt her arch into him once more and gasp. Only then did he allow himself to let go, and the two of them rolled over the precipice and into oblivion…

CHAPTER SEVEN

THAT night they slept naked and entwined around one another. And when they awoke in the morning they smiled drowsily into each other's eyes.

'Good morning, *cara mia*,' Ricardo whispered, drawing her closer to him and enjoying the feel of her body against his.

'Good morning,' Gabriella murmured, letting her head rest on his bare chest, closing her eyes again and basking in the knowledge that this was the first time she had ever awoken in a man's arms. It felt good, wonderful. She wished it could go on for ever.

'I have an idea,' Ricardo said, propping himself against the pillows and drawing her up beside him. 'Why don't we take the day off and go out on the yacht?'

'But I told the Contessa I would go with her to visit the orphanage this afternoon,' Gabriella said doubtfully, still letting her head rest lazily against his broad shoulder, lost in the scent of him, the rumpled sheets, and the tiny ache deep down in her core that proved to her that this was not a dream but a reality.

Ricardo tipped her chin up and dropped a kiss on her full lips. 'My beautiful Gabriella. I shall rearrange the schedule and all will be fine. Let me ring Alfredo and tell him to deal with it all. Then we must have breakfast—I'm ravenous.'

But before he could implement any of these plans Gabriella held him back. Slowly her fingers caressed his chest, roamed down to his stomach as she began to do her own investigation. Ricardo drew in his breath when her fingers, hesitant at first, gained confidence. Her lips began kissing his torso and her hand sought further. When at last she found him, felt the hardness of his desire and gently began to caress him, he let his eyes close and submitted to the delight. She was in-experienced, but her natural womanly instinct guided her where her knowledge was lacking. Soon Ricardo could bear it no longer. Quickly he took her in his arms, and unlike the night before, when he'd taken the time to prepare her, he thrust into her, knowing that she needed him as much as he needed her.

Together they feasted on one another, Gabriella's legs curling about his waist as he moved deep inside her, knowing that never before had he experienced such intensity with any woman. How extraordinary it was for this to happen with someone who had been thrown involuntarily into his path.

Gabriella wondered how she had ever lived without knowing the myriad sensations she had been exposed to in the past few hours. It was as though a new world had opened up before her, a window onto a new and wonderful scene that she had not known existed. And now he was asking her to spend the day with him, to go away together, as in quiet moments she'd allowed herself to dream that he would.

Half an hour later they were in the shower together, laughing as the water sprayed their bodies. Ricardo lathered soap on her back and Gabriella dropped the

shampoo, which bubbled up around them. Still laughing and kissing, they got out of the shower and dried
each other in huge terry towels embroidered with the
Maldoravian royal crest. Ricardo tied one around his
waist while Gabriella donned a bathrobe and they
headed back into the bedroom. Breakfast had been laid
out for them on the balcony.

'This is simply divine,' Gabriella said, stretching
and breathing in the fresh morning air as Ricardo came
up behind her and slipped his arms about her waist.

'Yes, Madame Wife, it is. Now, sit down and drink
your orange juice and have that croissant. You must
be hungry after so much activity.'

'That goes for you too,' she said, laughing and allowing him to pull out a wrought-iron chair for her to
sit on.

'I've ordered the yacht for eleven,' he said, glancing
at the time. 'That gives us an hour and a half. I'm
afraid I'll have to drop into the office for a few
minutes before we go.'

'I know.' She rolled her eyes. 'I'm getting used to
all the protocol, and to the fact that instead of being
a regal parasite living on the blood of your people
you're actually a very hard-working man.'

'Is that what you thought I was?' he asked curiously
as she spread jam on her croissant and let her white
teeth sink into it.

Gabriella shrugged. She had her mouth full so
couldn't answer.

At that moment the telephone rang and automatically Ricardo picked up. 'Yes, Alfredo. No, not today,'

An Important Message from the Editors

Dear Reader,

If you'd enjoy reading romance novels with larger print that's easier on your eyes, let us send you TWO FREE HARLEQUIN PRESENTS® NOVELS in our LARGER PRINT EDITION. These books are complete and unabridged, but the type is set about 20% bigger to make it easier to read. Look inside for an actual-size sample.

By the way, you'll also get a surprise gift with your two free books!

Pam Powers

Peel off Seal and Place Inside...

84

THE RIGHT WOMAN

she'd thought she was fine. It took Daniel's words and Brooke's question to make her realize she was far from a full recovery.

She'd made a start with her sister's help and she intended to go forward now. Sarah felt as if she'd been living in a darkened room and some-one had suddenly opened a door, letting in the fresh air and sunshine. She could feel its warmth slowly seeping into the coldest part of her. The feeling was liberating. She realized it was only a small step and she had a long way to go, but she was ready to face life again with Serena and her family behind her.

All too soon, they were saying goodbye and arah experienced a moment of sadness for all e years she and Serena had missed. But they d each other now and that's what d

She held a sy c

Printed in the U.S.A.
Publisher acknowledges the copyright holder of the excerpt from this individual work as follows:
THE RIGHT WOMAN Copyright © 2004 by Linda Warren. All rights reserved.
® and ™ are trademarks owned and used by the trademark owner and/or its licensee.

YOURS FREE!

You'll get a great mystery gift with
your two free larger print books!

GET TWO FREE
LARGER PRINT
BOOKS!

YES! Please send me two
free Harlequin Presents® novels
in the larger print edition, and
my free mystery gift, too. I
understand that I am under no
obligation to purchase
anything, as explained on the
back of this insert.

**PLACE
FREE GIFTS
SEAL
HERE**

◄ **DETACH AND MAIL CARD TODAY!** ►

106 HDL EFY5   306 HDL EFZH

FIRST NAME	LAST NAME

ADDRESS

APT.#	CITY

STATE/PROV.	ZIP/POSTAL CODE

**Are you a current Harlequin Presents® subscriber and
want to receive the larger print edition?**

Call 1-800-221-5011 today!

(H-PLPP-03/06) © 2004 Harlequin Enterprises Ltd.

The Harlequin Reader Service™ — Here's How It Works:

Accepting your 2 free Harlequin Presents® larger print books and gift places you under no obligation to buy anything. You may keep the books and gift and return the shipping statement marked "cancel." If you do not cancel, about a month later we'll send you 6 additional Harlequin Presents larger print books and bill you just $4.05 each in the U.S., or $4.72 each in Canada, plus 25¢ shipping & handling per book and applicable taxes if any.* That's the complete price and — compared to cover prices of $4.75 each in the U.S. and $5.50 each in Canada — it's quite a bargain! You may cancel at any time, but if you choose to continue, every month we'll send you 6 more books, which you may either purchase at the discount price or return to us and cancel your subscription.

*Terms and prices subject to change without notice. Sales tax applicable in N.Y. Canadian residents will be charged applicable provincial taxes and GST.

If offer card is missing write to: Harlequin Reader Service, 3010 Walden Ave., P.O. Box 1867, Buffalo, NY 14240-1867

BUSINESS REPLY MAIL
FIRST-CLASS MAIL   PERMIT NO. 717-003   BUFFALO, NY

POSTAGE WILL BE PAID BY ADDRESSEE

HARLEQUIN READER SERVICE
3010 WALDEN AVE
PO BOX 1867
BUFFALO NY 14240-9952

NO POSTAGE
NECESSARY
IF MAILED
IN THE
UNITED STATES

she heard him answer in the clipped, businesslike tones she was used to.

Gabriella smiled when their eyes met across the table. Ricardo's rolled heavenwards as the Baron went through a long list of obligations, but he stood firm. 'I'll deal with all that tomorrow, Alfredo. But today you must count me out. I'm spending it with my wife and shall not be available except in the case of a dire emergency.'

Ambrosia walked to the edge of the terrace of the stupendous Mediterranean villa which she had received as part of her second divorce settlement. She wore a long flowered silk kimono and held a glass of orange juice in her well-manicured hand. She was frowning as she stared out over the rocks and down to the yacht which was at present sailing into the harbour. It was the royal yacht. Was Ricardo preparing to sail? she wondered, taking a long sip of her juice.

Things were not been working out quite as she had planned. Ever since the beginning of their relationship she'd known there was only a very slight chance of her ever marrying Ricardo. That was pretty well out of the question. A twice-divorced woman was hardly suitable material for producing heirs to the Principality. Plus, if the truth be told, she had no desire to become a mother. The last thing she wanted was a pack of squawking brats to look after, and bearing them might ruin her perfect figure. But still, his sudden wedding, taking place as it had out of the blue, had caught her by surprise. It had not only angered her, it had set her nose out of joint. And Ambrosia was not used to this.

She had seen Ricardo's new wife for the first time at the club that day. That had been another shock. She had seen pictures in the papers, but nothing had prepared for the simple raw beauty the young girl possessed. In fact, she was far more beautiful and poised than Ambrosia had expected. And apparently sure of herself. That was what had disturbed Ambrosia the most: she had naturally assumed that a nineteen-year-old would be easily dealt with, that Ricardo would tire of the girl fast once he'd got her pregnant, that he would return to his mistress and her life would go back to having its previous pleasures. But there was no sign of this occurring, and as the days went by Ambrosia was becoming increasingly worried. Her friends had begun to tease her, some to make sly remarks.

This would not do, Ambrosia realised, watching the yacht's progress slow as it reached the harbour entrance. She must either decide to cut with Ricardo completely and find someone else, or make a stand.

As she finished off the last of the orange juice she inspected the mimosa. The gardener was not up to scratch, and she would complain to her housekeeper later on. But right now she was determined to find out exactly where the royal yacht was headed—and who would be sailing on her.

Inside, she sat at her antique desk and picked up the phone. She had contacts connected to the Palace—people who had made it their business to ingratiate themselves with her, as she had with them. She had done a few favours. Now she needed a small one in return.

'Hello? Is that Gian Carlo? How are you, darling?' she cooed down the phone.

'Ambrosia, darling.' The high-pitched male voice came back down the receiver. 'How wonderful to hear from you. You haven't been in to have your hair done. But of course that is understandable.'

'Isn't it?' she answered the hairdresser sweetly, pretending not to understand the meaning behind his words. 'I suppose you're doing you-know-who's hair now?'

'Actually, you're right, darling. I am. Quite gorgeous hair, actually,' he added.

'I'm sure. In the meantime, maybe you can tell me what the royal yacht is doing in the harbour and who is going on a trip?'

'Well, sweetie, I don't know all the details...' Gian Carlo's voice became almost a conspiratorial whisper. 'But I heard that this morning they were having breakfast on their balcony. Very gooey-eyed, if you know what I mean.'

'I know exactly what you mean,' Ambrosia said through gritted teeth. 'Go on.'

'Well, I overheard the secretary commenting that the Prince had asked for the yacht to be prepared for eleven. Apparently they're going out for a little romantic sea jaunt *à deux*.' He giggled shrilly and Ambrosia closed her eyes, determined not to allow her irritation to show.

'Thank you, Gian Carlo, darling,' she said instead. 'I'll be in soon. I need a trim and a manicure.'

'Of course, *bella*. Any time. And anything else you need to know,' he added with a purr, 'you can always count on me.'

'Of course I can, you nasty little creep,' she muttered, after slamming down the receiver. Eleven. That left her only an hour to strategise. Time to get moving.

With a swift sweeping movement she rose and marched up the stairs to her bedroom, her mind working at full throttle. This was a chance she wouldn't miss. She would put him against the wall, whether he liked it or not.

And that cool little bitch of a wife of his with him.

Gabriella slipped on her bikini, a short pink cotton skirt with a matching top and pink ballerina shoes, and headed jauntily down the large staircase with her bag over her shoulder, happier than she had been since setting foot in the Palace. The whole place looked different this morning—brighter, jollier. Even the servants, who always seemed pretty stiff and formal, appeared more likeable. She said bright good mornings to everyone she passed before popping her head around the door of the Contessa's apartment to see if she was in.

'Hello, my love. You look very well and pretty this morning,' the Contessa remarked, tipping her gold-framed glasses down her nose and inspecting Gabriella closely.

'Yes,' she said, letting out a breath and smiling happily. 'I'm sorry that I had to cancel our trip to the orphanage. Ricardo and I are taking the day off. We're going to sail away all day, just the two of us.'

'How lovely,' the Contessa exclaimed, smiling be-
nevolently, hoping that at last things were beginning
to take on a new shape. Perhaps the couple had finally
found common ground. She certainly hoped so, for not
only did she like Gabriella very much, she could not
have imagined a lovelier, more perfect wife for
Ricardo—even if the girl was younger than she would
have chosen.

'Well, I'd better be off. I just popped in to say
hello.' Gabriella deposited a warm kiss on the older
woman's cheek and left, skipping down the rest of the
steps to where Ricardo's Ferrari stood parked, waiting
for them. She looked up at the Palace, anxious for him
to join her. Perhaps, she thought, taking a deep breath,
they would make love again on the boat. Just the
thought of spending all day lying in his arms soaking
up the sun and the sea was delicious.

She didn't have to wait long before Ricardo appeared, casually dressed in white jeans and a navy
T-shirt, a sweater flung over his shoulders.

'Ready?' he said, winking at her as they jumped
into his car, and he took off down the gracious driveway and out onto the road.

Gabriella couldn't stop smiling as they drove down
through the old town towards the harbour. Ricardo had
dispensed with his security guards today, which he
often did in Maldoravia. In fact, he was often to be
found wandering about quite happily among the people—to the horror of his security team, who went
crazy trying to keep track of him. It felt so good to
feel the wind blowing her hair, see the people going
about their business, the old men leading donkeys with

baskets laden with flowers and fresh fruit, small children with their mothers in brightly clad clothes, some of whom waved at them, smiling.

Then they were entering the Royal Yacht Club marina, where the royal yacht lay out at anchor, for she was too big to dock.

They left the car with the club valet and went inside.

'I guess we might have time for a quick drink,' Ricardo remarked. 'It's only ten to eleven.'

'Okay.' Gabriella was on for anything right now. Just looking at him, knowing she'd spent the night in his arms, left her weak with longing for more, and as they sat next to each other on the terrace she had to hold back from extending her hand and taking his.

'Well, well—what a surprise.'

Suddenly a shadow extended over them and Gabriella looked up. She immediately recognised the woman she'd seen that day at this club a couple of months earlier. She saw the way the woman looked at Ricardo and a shiver ran through her.

'Ambrosia, hello.' Ricardo rose politely. 'May I introduce you to my wife? Gabriella, this is an old friend of mine—Ambrosia de la Fuente.'

'Delighted to meet you,' Ambrosia cooed, taking in every detail of Gabriella's outfit and making the latter feel as if somehow she'd got herself dirty.

'Hello.' Gabriella took her hand and experienced another shiver, as though she'd touched a snake. She hastily withdrew it.

'Won't you sit down?' Ricardo was saying.

To her horror, Gabriella watched as the woman accepted his invitation and slid sensually into the vacant chair next to him. Her slinky tall figure seemed to vibrate with sex appeal, and she made Gabriella feel young and gauche and inexperienced, a sensation she had rarely had before. Normally she was quite self-confident, but for some reason this woman left her ill at ease. She watched as Ambrosia ordered a cocktail and Ricardo joined her, and felt stupid having ordered a cola. Determined not to allow herself to be made to feel inferior, Gabriella plastered on a bright smile and tried to join in the conversation.

'Do you live here in Maldoravia?' she asked politely as the waiter served their drinks.

'Not too much salt in this margarita, I hope, Pepe?' Ambrosia said, ignoring Gabriella's question and turning to the waiter, who bowed graciously and murmured that he hoped madam's drink would be to her satisfaction. Ambrosia took a small sexy sip, then allowed her tongue to slide over her upper lip. 'It's perfect,' she said with a condescending smile at the young man. Then she turned back to Gabriella.

'You were saying?' Her expression was as haughty as when she had been dealing with the waiter.

'I was asking if you lived here,' Gabriella replied, trying to control her temper. This woman was making a conscious effort to make her feel bad.

'Actually, I used to spend quite a lot of time here,' Ambrosia answered, casting a quick sidelong smile at Ricardo. 'Whether I will or not in the future depends on a number of things.'

'Ah.' There was really not much to say.

At that moment a group of sophisticated young people in their late twenties and early thirties entered the club. Immediately they waved and came over to the table.

'Hello, Ricky! Ambrosia, darling, it's been an age,' one of the women said, kissing Ricardo and then leaning over to peck Ambrosia on the cheek. 'How wonderful to see both of you.'

Gabriella watched as they all chatted and laughed, feeling increasingly embarrassed and humiliated. Ricardo was turning towards her now, and introducing her to one of the men. She smiled automatically and watched as Ambrosia carried on an animated conversation, referring to people Gabriella had never met and places she had never heard of. It was with a sigh of relief that she saw the yacht's first mate approaching. Surely he must be coming to say that the vessel was ready for them to embark? At last they would leave behind this crowd of superficial socialites, who were fast getting on her nerves, and then the day would go back to being perfect.

'Ricky, are you going out for a sail?' asked one of the men—Peter something-or-other; she hadn't caught his last name.

'Actually, yes. I'm taking the day off.' Ricardo smiled over at Gabriella, who got ready to take her leave.

'But, Rick, you're not going out alone, are you? How dreadfully boring! Why, we can't let that happen—can we, gang?' protested one of the women, a small, lively brunette in large designer sunglasses, laughing.

'Absolutely not,' Ambrosia chipped in, tipping her shades and looking over the rim at Ricardo, her eyes alive with amusement and challenge. 'I can't think of anything more deadly than going out alone with one's husband. Poor Gabriella,' she said, turning and smiling triumphantly.

Gabriella was about to retort when, to her horror, she heard Ricardo inviting the group to join them. At that moment her eyes flew to his, but he had transformed into the perfect urbane host, offering the yacht and his hospitality. There was no sign of the smouldering embers that had been there only hours before.

Her heart sank and she had to stifle a sudden rush of tears. Only her pride held her together. But it was too unfair. The one day she had with him, the one time they could be alone, to consolidate all that had taken place last night, was being ripped from her by this dreadful woman whom she already detested. Her and her awful friends. She felt young and silly and out of it. And she hated Ricardo for giving in to them all so easily, for not preserving what he should have realised was so important.

Two hours later the *Blue Mermaid* approached the small ancient walled town of Travania. It was a charming, beautiful place that Gabriella had heard of but as yet had not visited. It was a historical gem, according to the guidebooks, a place that had known Roman settlers, Ottoman rule, a crossroads of cultures. How she would have loved to visit the place alone with Ricardo.

But that was out of the question. There were at least ten people on board. Drinks were being served, and as they anchored off the coast of Travania lunch was being prepared. Gabriella tried to keep up the best front she could—chatting brightly with several of the crowd, forcing herself not to judge them—while wishing them a million miles away. The worst was seeing her husband ensconced in a long conversation with Ambrosia up on the front deck. They were alone and talking intently. Gabriella watched them a moment— watched the intimate way in which they leaned towards one another—certain now that by some unknown means the woman had planned the whole thing. Reason told her that it was impossible, that it was just a coincidence—there was no way anybody could have known about their planned boating trip. But something about Ambrosia and the hard confidence she exuded told her otherwise.

Gabriella felt a shiver run through her. She must find out the truth, must know what her relationship with Ricardo was. And the only people who would tell her the truth were the Contessa or Constanza. After all, she barely knew any other women, had no girlfriends to speak of, and could hardly consult with Baron Alfredo on the matter.

With a sigh, Gabriella leaned on the yacht's railing and stared down into the deep.

'A penny for your thoughts?'

'Oh.' She looked up to see Peter, the handsome young Englishman who'd joined the party at the club, smiling down at her.

'Well?'

'Oh, nothing, really. Just looking at the water, that's all,' she lied.

'I don't think that's quite true,' Peter answered with a winning smile. 'You know, I imagine that suddenly becoming Princess and having to deal with a new life can't be altogether easy.' He spoke sympathetically.

'Uh, no, you're right. It's not. But one gets used to it.'

'In two months? That's pretty good. Particularly when your husband spends half his time working.'

Gabriella tensed and then stiffened. 'My husband does all he can to help me,' she said, her chin tilting upwards.

'That's very sweet and loyal,' Peter said in a soft voice. 'I like seeing a woman stick up for her man. Even when that man doesn't deserve it,' he added dryly, glancing towards the forward deck.

Gabriella's eyes followed his. She bit her lip. She could not ask this man for the truth. Would not subject herself to that humiliation. If it was true, and Ambrosia was Ricardo's mistress, then everyone on this boat knew and she must be a laughing stock.

Then suddenly Gabriella realised that if that was the case it really didn't matter what Peter thought of her, and that she might as well learn the truth.

'Ambrosia is Ricardo's mistress, isn't she?' she said, in a low voice that tried to sound off-hand, as if this sort of thing happened every day.

Peter hesitated. He was a nice man, who had not realised to what extent Ambrosia was prepared to push things and manipulate situations to get Ricardo back. As soon as he'd seen what was going on he'd felt ashamed at being a part of her dirty tricks and causing this lovely young girl problems.

'Please,' Gabriella said, gripping the railing, 'I know I must seem like the world's biggest idiot to you, but do me a favour and don't leave me in the dark. They sleep together, don't they?'

'Did,' he answered quickly. 'I don't believe that since your marriage they have been together. I think that is why Ambrosia staged this whole thing—to see if she could try and get Ricardo to go back to her.'

'Well,' Gabriella said, with a bright smile and a glance in the direction of the two, 'she seems to be doing a pretty good job, doesn't she?'

'I don't think so. You shouldn't worry about Ambrosia. She's history and she knows it. How could she be anything else when Ricardo's got you?'

'Ha!' Gabriella exclaimed with a bitter laugh. 'Do you think I'm so young and inexperienced that I don't know what links a man and a woman? You just have to look at them to know there is something more than just friendship—' The words caught in her throat and she turned and swallowed.

'Gabriella, don't,' Peter said, taking her hand impulsively. 'I hate to see you like this. It's not fair of either of them to put you through this. But don't worry. I'll see what I can do.'

'No, you won't do anything of the sort,' Gabriella remonstrated, whirling around, her eyes blazing. 'You will leave it well alone. This is my problem, not yours. Or rather it is Ricardo's problem, and my problem, and that woman's. If he wants to sleep with her, then he's welcome to her. I don't care.'

Turning, she pulled her hand from his grasp, hurried away and went downstairs to the stateroom, where she sat on the bed and took a deep breath. She should have known last night was nothing but an illusion—his way of securing her womanhood, his way of putting his stamp on her—and nothing more. She hoped the day would go by fast and that soon she could get back to Maldoravia. At least there she would be in the privacy of her own apartments and would not be made a public spectacle. From now on, she knew the truth and would not be made a fool of any longer.

He would never touch her again.

Not as long as he lived.

Not if she had anything to do with it.

CHAPTER EIGHT

'DID you have a nice day?' the Contessa asked next morning, as she and Gabriella sat in the back of the limousine on their way to visit the orphanage.

'It was all right, thank you,' she replied blankly.

The Contessa took a sidelong glance at the girl. Gone was the glow of yesterday. In its stead she saw tenseness, dark rings under her eyes and a deep sadness surrounding her. What on earth could have gone wrong in such a short time? she asked herself. She must try and get the girl to confide in her. Something was definitely not right.

Ricardo sat behind the large antique desk in his office and thought about the previous day. What a disaster. He should have known Ambrosia would set him up. At least he'd taken the opportunity to make it abundantly plain to her that their relationship was most definitely over and that there would be no more nocturnal visits to her house. He should have done that before he got married, he realised. But how could he have guessed that making love to Gabriella would be such a magical experience? He had never imagined that anything could turn into the night before last.

But he would rather not remember last night. Gone had been the loving, beautiful creature of the night before, the enchanting woman whom he'd breakfasted with. In her stead had been an angry, capricious teen-ager who had ranted at him for having his friends on board. He had considered telling her the truth, but thought better of it. If she didn't know about the past and Ambrosia then there was no point in opening up Pandora's box.

'I'm sorry about today,' he'd said as they returned to the Palace last evening. 'I wanted to spend it alone with you, but it would have been impossible to refuse my friends a ride.'

'That has become abundantly clear,' Gabriella threw at him angrily. 'Another time just tell me you prefer their company to mine and I'll stay behind.'

'Gabriella, stop being childish.'

'Childish, am I? Okay, then, have it your way. Maybe I am childish—or just plain stupid. You obviously had a good time.'

'What do you mean?' he asked guardedly as they swung into the Palace driveway.

'Nothing. I didn't mean anything. And I really don't want to talk to you any more.'

She had jumped out of the car and made her way quickly up the stairs, and he hadn't seen her again all evening. She'd sent a message saying she had a head-ache and would not be dining with him, and when he'd come to bed only the nightlight had been on and she'd either been fast asleep or pretended to be.

This morning he'd tried to raise the subject with her. But instead of fury he'd encountered cold, icy indif-ference. And to his surprise it had hurt.

Now, as he fiddled with his pen and ignored the pile of letters he needed to sign, he thought about her and the night spent with her in his arms. And all at once he knew that he wanted to save this marriage that had taken them both so by surprise.

He would have to find a way of making her fall in love with him.

But the next few days gave no opportunities for his plan to develop. First he was called away to a state funeral in the Middle East, then on his way back he had to make a trip to Bahrain, followed by a few hectic days dealing with some business affairs in London and Paris. When he phoned the Palace he received the news that his wife had gone to join his sister at her *schloss* in Austria.

After some deliberation, he decided to go and pay his sister a surprise visit.

The towered Austrian *schloss* was like a building out of a Grimm's fairy tale—all towers and small mullioned windows and perfectly enchanting. But, although summer was lovely by the Wolfgang See, with small boats puttering on the mirror-like lake, children swimming and playing at the water's edge, Gabriella found little to be happy about. Her one joy was being with Constanza's children, whom she adored. The affection was reciprocated. They didn't want to go anywhere without her. Now, on the *schloss*'s private beach, she lay on a chaise longue and watched little Anita and Ricky splashing in the water. Their nanny stood close by, supervising, and Constanza drooped languidly, a large sunhat covering her face in the next chaise longue.

'What gorgeous weather. I'm so pleased it's held.

And I'm glad that you decided to come and stay, Gabriella. I wonder if Ricardo will think of joining us.'

'I doubt it,' she replied dryly. 'He's far too busy to spend any time relaxing.'

'Do you think so?' Constanza tipped up her hat and took a surreptitious look at her sister-in-law. The girl was tense, and looked positively haggard at times. What was her brother up to?

From the first moment she had set eyes on Gabriella, just before the wedding, she'd been convinced that this might just be the making of him. He might finally get rid of that dreadful Mexican woman, whom she loathed. Over the years Ricardo had had a number of girlfriends and mistresses, some of whom had been friends. Others, like Ambrosia, had been a real pain in the butt. Serve her right that Ricardo had gone off and suddenly married a girl fourteen years his junior, who was not only stunningly beautiful but struck her as intelligent to boot.

'You don't seem to spend much time with Ricardo,' she remarked, picking up her water bottle and taking a long sip.

'He is always very occupied.'

'Gabriella, I hate to interfere, and please tell me to stop if I'm being intrusive, but it strikes me that all is not well with you and Ricardo. And what's more,' she added perceptively, 'you have no one to talk to about it. I assure you that anything you say here will remain strictly confidential—even though I am his sister.'

Gabriella stiffened and she sat up straighter, tears knotted in her throat. 'I—I don't really know. I...'

Then to her horror she broke down, and tears poured down her cheeks.

Constanza jumped up and sat next to her, grabbing her hands. 'Oh, you poor darling. What has he done, the monster? I promise you he will regret it. You don't deserve to be unhappy.'

'It's not his f-fault,' she muttered through her tears. 'We only got married because my father insisted when he was dying. He made me promise. It was unfair to both of us, but there was no way out. If Ricardo hadn't married me I would have lost my entire fortune. So, you see, there was no love involved. He was just being a gentleman, I suppose. I hate the way things are between us, but the truth is he did his duty and I guess it's only normal that now he wants his old life back.'

'I don't believe it,' Constanza exclaimed, amazed. 'It is obvious that he cares for you, Gabriella. You just have to see the way he looks at you.'

'You think so?' Gabriella looked up, her eyes swimming. She sniffed loudly and searched for a hanky. 'There was one time when I—I thought that perhaps… But then—' She broke off, remembering the wonderful night followed by the awful day on the yacht.

'But then what?' Constanza prodded, frowning.

'Then Ambrosia appeared, with all her horrid friends, and it was simply awful. I thought we were going to spend the day together, but he preferred to spend it with her. They are obviously very intimate. That much was blatant,' she added, clenching her fists and gritting her teeth.

'Well? You're not going to let him get away with it, are you?'

'What do you mean?'

'Mean? Why, give as good as you get, of course,' the other woman exclaimed with a laugh. 'If he's encouraging that creature then you'd better let him know that there are lots of men after you.'

'Yes, well, that's all very well,' Gabriella responded dourly, 'but there aren't. And even if there were I would never encourage them. After all, I'm a married woman now. It wouldn't be right.'

'Big deal,' Constanza scoffed. 'Of course you wouldn't go as far as having an affair with anyone, but a little flirtation—just enough to make Ricardo jealous—would do him no harm at all, don't you think?'

'I don't know. Do you really think it would work?' Gabriella turned her face up to her sister-in-law, the idea taking root.

'I absolutely do.'

'But I don't know any men. Plus, surely it would be wrong and make me appear—well, vulgar, and...'

'Leave it to me,' Constanza said grandly. 'I shall organise the whole thing.'

'But—'

'Trust me. Just be prepared to look beautiful and be at your most charming,' she answered with a smug, mischievous smile. 'We'll see if it doesn't do the trick.'

The helicopter ride from Munich airport took barely twenty minutes, and as the chopper prepared to land Ricardo looked down at the lake, at the peaceful scene below, glad he'd decided to come. Maybe here he and

Gabriella could get off to a fresh start. They certainly needed to if anything was going to come of this marriage.

When the chopper landed he saw his sister coming out of the castle and stepping onto the lawn, waving. He'd called her earlier, to tell her he planned to arrive and not to tell Gabriella. When she hadn't sounded surprised at his visit, he'd smiled. Constanza knew him pretty well.

Brother and sister embraced and moved towards the house, Ricardo carrying a large tote bag which he laid down in the hall.

'How is Wilhelm?' he asked.

'Fine. He'll be back from Salzburg very shortly.'

'And where is Gabriella?' he asked.

'Oh, she's off somewhere,' Constanza replied with studied vagueness. 'Why don't you come onto the terrace and have a glass of lemonade? The heat is unbearable.'

'I'd love to. But where is my wife?'

'I told you—she went out.'

'Where?' he insisted.

'I have Ruddy Hofstetten and Jamie Reid-Harper staying. They all seem to be getting along rather well together. Ruddy asked Gabriella to go biking with them.'

'Ruddy Hofstetten? You must be kidding? What the hell is he doing here?' Ricardo frowned.

'He and Jamie asked if they could spend a few days here. As they're both good friends of Wilhelm's brother Franz, of course we agreed. Actually,' she said slyly, 'I think it's been rather nice for Gabriella to have some young people around her. She seems to spend so much time on her own. Ah, here's the lemonade,' Constanza added, glancing at Ricardo out of the corner of her eye to see how he'd reacted to the news that one of Europe's most notorious playboys happened to be staying.

Ricardo said nothing, merely sat down on the charming terrace and looked about him. 'You have done a lovely job on this place, Constanza. Very tasteful indeed.'

'Mmm.' Constanza had no desire to talk about her decorating skills. Instead, she hoped he would open up about his marriage. But she doubted that would happen. Ricardo and she had always got on well together but he always kept his private life exactly that: private.

Well, she'd done all she could, had primed the boys, and now she hoped that her plan would work. And, actually, Ricardo might really have to be careful. She had merely intended that the young men's visit be nothing but a ploy. But it had immediately been obvious that Gabriella's beauty and charm was not lost on either of them. Time would tell how Ricardo would react to seeing his wife being the centre of so much male attention, she figured, pouring lemonade from the crystal jug with a private smile.

'Oh, it's great fun,' Gabriella exclaimed as the two Harley Davidson bikes rolled up, stopping in front of the *schloss*. She alighted. 'Thanks, Ruddy. I enjoyed every minute of the trip. Can we go again tomorrow?'

'Your wish is my command, Princess,' the dashing young count replied, tossing his long blond hair back and loosening the leather jacket that he wore for biking.

'Oh, please, don't call me that. It makes me feel ancient.'

'Okay, Gabriella, then. It is a very pretty name, and it suits you rather well,' he said in his smooth sexy voice.

'We could take a picnic,' she murmured, unbuttoning her jacket.

'We could. On the other hand, I have a better idea.'

'Oh?' She looked up, smiling, her eyes sparkling. She hadn't had so much fun in a while.

'I have the perfect spot for us to lunch. Hey, Jamie,' Ruddy said, turning towards his friend, who was getting off his bike and coming to join them. 'Do you remember that delightful little *heurigen* we went to last year?'

'Yes. It wasn't far south of here. I'm sure we could find it again. Or maybe Constanza will remember. Well, Gabi,' he said, sending Gabriella a teasing smile, 'did you enjoy your first motorbike ride?'

'It wasn't my first ride,' she scoffed, tossing her head back with a mischievous smile. 'My father was a great motorcyclist. I went all over South America with him on the back of a bike.'

'Ah! A veteran, I see. That's great. Maybe we can persuade Constanza to join us tomorrow. Here—help me pull these gloves off, will you?' He held out his hands for Gabriella to tug.

Laughing, she pulled at the gloves, which were rather tight. Jamie pulled back and she fell into his arms.

'Oh, sorry,' she cried breathlessly.

'I can handle mistakes like these,' Jamie said smoothly, grinning down at her, a twinkle in his eye.

Gabriella flushed and, recovering her balance, turned away. Then she looked up. 'Oh, my God,' she whispered, a flush rushing to her cheeks.

'Hello, Gabriella,' Ricardo said, coming down the steps in a casual manner and nodding to her two companions. 'Hello, Ruddy. I haven't seen you about in a while or you for that matter, Jamie. How is your father?'

'Better, thanks,' Jamie replied.

The three men took stock of each other while Gabriella tried to compose herself. What on earth was Ricardo doing here? He hadn't told her he was coming—hadn't even given her an inkling. Had he seen her fall into Jamie's arms? She knew Constanza wanted her to flirt with other men in his presence, but between flirting and being embraced there was a difference. She turned her flushed face towards him, a sudden shudder scaring through her when slipped his arm around her and his lips met hers in a brief encounter.

'Hello, my dear. I thought I'd pay you all a surprise visit.'

'Yes. Well, it is a surprise. We weren't expecting you. I—' She stopped, smiled, and looked down.

'Apparently not,' he murmured.

Minutes later they were heading up the wide oak staircase and down a large corridor filled with empty suits of armour, its walls graced by portraits of

Wilhelm's ancestors, to the suite of rooms Constanza had allotted them.

'I had no idea you were coming to visit,' Gabriella said, to make conversation as they entered the room.

'No. I gathered that.'

'What do you mean?' she asked, posing her gloves on the chest of drawers and taking off the leather clothes she'd borrowed from Constanza for the bike trip.

'Merely that you seemed to be having a good time and probably weren't too concerned about my whereabouts.'

'Should I have been concerned?' she asked coolly.

'I don't know. That depends how much you care whether I'm near you or not.'

His eyes bored into hers and she looked away, unwilling to let him see just how much his presence affected her. She would not go through another humiliation, she reminded herself, remembering the incident at the yacht club and its aftermath.

'I think you're teasing,' she said at last, picking up her silk dressing gown and heading towards the bathroom.

'Wait, Gabriella. I want to speak to you.'

'Yes?' She turned and looked at him expectantly, trying not to show by her expression just how handsome she thought he looked in a pair of stonewashed jeans and a white T-shirt, so casual compared to how he was usually attired.

'Gabriella, I want to talk to you about the future.'

Her heart skipped a beat. 'This is hardly the right moment. I'm about to take a shower. I was out on a bike all day and I don't think that—' She broke off as he crossed the room and planted his hands on her shoulders.

'When is the right time, in your view?'

'I—I don't know. What I mean to say is—'

'That you would prefer not to have to talk to me at all? That you much prefer the company of young playboys like Ruddy and Jamie?' There was an edge to his voice and his grip on her shoulders tightened.

'I don't know what you mean,' she murmured, staring at his chest.

'I think you do. You look happier than I've seen you in a while. Do you plan to separate from me in a few months' time and begin a relationship with one of them?'

'How can you say such a thing?' she exclaimed, staring up at him, her eyes ablaze with righteous anger. Then she remembered Constanza's advice and, looking away, she countered. 'Of course if that is the way you would prefer things to be, then why not?' She shrugged, pretended to be indifferent, and had the pleasure of seeing his expression darken, his thick brows meet over the bridge of his patrician nose. His hands dropped from her shoulders and he looked down at her.

'I see. So I was right after all.'

'Right about what?'

'Right that you have forgotten this,' he said, his hands snaking to her waist and drawing her close against him. 'You may find Ruddy and his cohorts attractive, *cara mia*, but you are still my wife,' he said

bitingly. 'And I would appreciate it if you didn't forget it.'

His lips clamped down on hers before she could
move or do more than give a tiny muffled cry of protest that was silenced as his tongue worked its way
cleverly on hers. Heat soared to her core, leaving her
limp and wanting. What was it about this man that she
couldn't resist? In a hazy blur Gabriella allowed her
arms to entwine about his neck and obediently followed him as he pulled her over to the bed. She
dropped the dressing gown in a heap on the floor.
Soon the rest of their clothes followed and Ricardo
drew her into his arms, on top of him, so that she lay
draped over him. He held her tight, pressing her ab-
domen to his, making her feel the rush of desire con-
suming him.

Gabriella looked down into his eyes, her lips parted
and a new sense of her own sexuality suddenly taking
hold. All at once she felt powerful and in control.
Instead of embarrassment she felt triumph as slowly
she moved on top of him, easing herself until he thrust
inside her with a groan. Then slowly her hips began
to rotate. Ricardo gripped her waist. It was wonderful
to feel him deep inside her, to know that she was the
one controlling the situation, determining the rhythm
of their lovemaking, to know that he lay there at her
mercy.

Then, just as she was testing her skills, Ricardo
lifted her off him in one swift movement and, revers-
ing their positions, drove himself inside her, leaving
her panting and longing. Now he was the one calling
the shots, and she lay back with a little cry of ecstasy

as he loved her, easing in and out of her until she could
bear it no longer, until she begged him to bring her to
completion. When she thought she could stand it no
longer he drove her further, until at last they climaxed
together, falling among the rumpled sheets, exhausted.

Ricardo lay back, his head against the pillows, his eyes
closed. Not in many years had he experienced the rush
of sensuality that Gabriella caused. Lovemaking for
him over the past few years had been an expert form
of exercise—a pastime he'd indulged in with sophisticated, well-versed women like Ambrosia, who'd
made sure they highlighted his preferences and pan-
dered to his tastes. But with Gabriella all that had
changed. This was raw, sensual lovemaking such as
he had not known for ages—if ever, he recognised,
shocked at how off balance she made him. The sight
of her laughing up at Jamie had left him hot with a
raw new sensation that he now recognised as jealousy.
He had never felt jealous of any woman before. Had
never needed to. Mostly women made sure they were
exactly what he wanted them to be. And when things
burned out, as they usually did after a while, it was
all very civilised. Each of them moved on and they
remained friends.

But this was different. He knew all at once that he
could never remain simply friends with Gabriella. That
would be impossible. Every time he looked at her he
envisaged her as she was now, her beautiful sensual
body lying naked among the sheets. His body; his
woman. He would never let any other man touch her,
he vowed, his fist clenching.

Then he turned and watched her, reaching down and dropping a kiss on the tip of her perfect young breast. When he sucked it she gasped.

'No, please, Ricardo. Not again. I don't think I could. I—' .

'Mmm.' Ricardo paid no attention, simply continued to draw the soft nipple into his mouth, grazing it with his teeth, laving it until Gabriella thought she would die of sheer delight. Again the ache between her thighs mounted. She had thought only moments ago that she was saturated, could not move. Yet here she was, her hips arching, her hands seeking him, reaching out to him with all her being as once again they found one another.

Ricardo slid inside her, not hungrily or tempestuously as he had earlier, but softly and smoothly, as though completing something, sending her a message that said *I possess you in every way and you will not escape me.*

And the truth was that right then she didn't want to.

CHAPTER NINE

DINNER was served on the terrace. Champagne and delicious Austrian wines accompanied the meal. Conversation flowed and the ambience was delightful. For the first time since she'd known her husband Gabriella saw Ricardo really at ease. He laughed with them, told amusing stories, captivated his audience and was altogether different from the autocratic being she'd become so used to.

'So. What about tomorrow?' Ruddy asked, once they were all sitting in wicker chairs drinking coffee and partaking of after-dinner drinks. The moonlight reflected on the lake, sending a fine shimmering silver across the peaceful waters.

'What about tomorrow?' Ricardo rejoined.

'We are going on another bike trip. Want to come along?'

'Where to?'

'We thought we'd head south, maybe stop by one of the other lakes for lunch.'

'I really ought to be leaving tomorrow,' he replied. 'And you should be coming home too, Gabriella. There are several engagements that require your presence in Maldoravia.'

'But, Ricky, this is the summer vacation. Gabriella's having fun. Don't spoil it.'

'That wasn't my intention,' he said stiffly. 'Of course, if she wants to stay that is different.'

He looked across at Gabriella, sitting between Constanza and Jamie. 'Well?' His tone implied that he expected her to obey him.

A sudden flash of anger gripped her. Just because she succumbed to him in bed it did not mean she was going to let herself be treated like some nineteenth-century wife.

'I think I'll stay. I promised the children that I would take them fishing. I would hate to disappoint them.'

A look passed between Ruddy and Jamie. It was not lost on Ricardo. He was about to make a pithy comment, then pressed his lips shut. 'Very well. As you wish. I'm rather tired,' he added, getting up and altering the mood as he took his brandy snifter with him. 'If you'll excuse me, Constanza, I think I'll finish this upstairs and get ready for an early night. I'll order the chopper for seven-thirty.'

'I'm damned if I'm having that noise on the lawn so early,' his sister protested. 'Seven-thirty, indeed. How uncivilised, Ricky. No wonder Gabriella wants to stay, if you're being unbearable.'

She was caught in a web. On the one hand she would have loved to be with Ricardo. But his whole attitude was so domineering and arrogant. *Insupportable* was the word that came to mind. He really believed that because she was his for the taking in bed she would simply comply with his every wish. Well, she wasn't leaving and that was that, Gabriela decided, as she dressed to go on the excursion. There was no sign of Ricardo, who appeared to have left early. But she had heard nothing, and if a helicopter had landed then she'd slept through the noise.

At nine-thirty she descended to the large dining room, where breakfast was being served.

'Ah, there you are.' Constanza smiled and indicated to her to sit down. 'I didn't hear Ricardo leave, did you?'

'No, I didn't. Maybe he left by car.'

'I'll ask Hans the butler when he comes in. He must have seen him. So, are you off with the boys for the day?'

'Yes. Though it's a pity the weather doesn't look too great.'

'No,' Constanza agreed as Gabriella sat down. She passed her the toast. 'The forecast announced intermittent showers. You'd better take something to cover up, just in case.'

'I will. I'm really looking forward to it.'

'Good morning.'

Ruddy and Jamie entered the dining room, looking handsome and ready for the day's fun.

'We've got the bikes all set, and we thought we'd be off before eleven. Is that okay with you, Gabi?'

'Fine. Constanza says the weather may turn bad.'

'Think so?' Ruddy went to the window and peered out. 'It's a bit cloudy, but nothing to worry about. If it starts raining we can stop off somewhere and have a drink or something.'

'Sounds good,' Jamie said, joining the ladies at the table and tucking in to a large plate of ham and eggs.

At eleven sharp the three were ready to go. Gabriella mounted the back of Ruddy's bike and Jamie drove alone. Soon they were heading along the pretty lakeside road, and Gabriella clung tight to Ruddy's waist as the bike gained speed and they whizzed around corners, then slowed to go through picturesque villages, with little white houses, painted shutters and people walking around in traditional dress—the girls in dirndles and the men in traditional suede jackets and green feathered hats.

An hour later they were well into the Tyrol. The clouds that earlier had seemed light now hung low and dark in the sky, and a rumble of thunder could be heard in the distance.

'Let's stop for a bite of lunch. I think that place is only a little further on,' Jamie called as they rode side by side on the empty road.

'Right.'

Ten minutes later they drew up at a small hotel on the banks of a lake. Outside long tables were laid, and a big array of smoked meats, cheeses and delicacies was spread on a large wooden table adorned with a bright chequered red and white cloth.

'This is lovely,' Gabriella exclaimed, removing her helmet and shaking out the long black hair that poured over her shoulders. Then she took off her jacket and looked up at the sky. 'A bit risky to stay outside, don't you think?'

'Oh, I think we just might manage lunch,' Ruddy said, his eyes following hers. As she sat down he gave her a speculative glance, but said nothing.

Once installed at the *heurigen* they ordered cold meat, cheese and sausage and a bottle of Weltliner, the local wine. Ruddy kept filling her glass, letting his hand lie next to hers.

'Look, I want to go and visit a friend of mine who lives a few miles from here,' Jamie remarked, pouring them another glass. 'Would you mind if we split up and meet again in Graz?'

'No, that's fine,' Ruddy answered carelessly.

'Do you think that's wise?' Gabriella asked. The clouds were growing darker, and some people were beginning to head indoors. 'You might get caught in the rain.'

'Don't worry about me, gorgeous,' Jamie said, getting up and winking at her. 'I'll be fine. I'll see you in a while. Give me a buzz on the mobile when you're through,' he murmured to Ruddy.

Gabriella frowned. It sounded almost as if this were a planned thing between them. But she shrugged it off. 'I suppose we should get going too.'

'Oh, no, not yet. We've got lots of time. Anyway, it's rather fun biking in the rain. But first I want to show you this place properly. It's very old and charming. Dates back to the sixteenth century, actually.'

Gabriella experienced a moment's hesitation which she immediately banished. 'I'd love to.'

'Right. Well, why don't we finish this wine, then I'll give you a guided tour?'

A few minutes later Ruddy was leading Gabriella indoors. He spoke in German to the lady behind the desk, who beamed at him and handed him a key.

'What's that for?' Gabriella asked curiously.

'Oh, she thought you might like to see one of the suites. They're beautifully decorated. All in the original style of the region.'

'That would be very nice,' Gabriella said, smiling at the woman and following Ruddy up the creaking wooden staircase, delighted by the small crooked windows with their ruffled curtains, and the scent of pot pourri. The place was truly charming.

At the top of the stairs Ruddy stopped, then turned right. 'Here it is,' he said, unlocking a large hand-painted door at the end of the corridor. 'This is the

prettiest suite in the house. Come in and take a look.'
He opened the door for her and stood aside for her to
enter.

Gabriella stepped inside and was enchanted. The
small living room had been beautifully decorated with
wooden furniture piled with red and green cushions,
all in Austrian patterns. A fireplace stood in the centre
of the room, and through the windows at the far end
was a magnificent view over the Alps. 'It's perfectly
gorgeous,' she exclaimed, moving towards the window.

'And come and see this,' Ruddy urged, taking her
arm and leading her towards the bedroom, where a
huge antique four-poster graced the room 'Isn't that
delightful?'

'Yes, it is. Thanks for bringing me here and showing me all of this,' she answered, turning around and
smiling at him.

'No need to thank me, beautiful,' he responded, his
voice turning low and husky. 'I thought that we might
just spend a little time here together. I've been thinking of nothing else since the moment I met you,
Gabriella.' He reached out and to her shock pulled her
into his arms.

'Ruddy, no—this is ridiculous. I—'

'Shush,' he teased, stroking her hair, slipping his
hand to the back of her neck and tilting her head back.
'Just relax and enjoy it. It'll be a change from that
pokered-up husband of yours. He must be a royal pain
in the ass,' he muttered, laughing before bringing his
mouth down on hers.

Gabriella felt a moment's panic. Then she began to
struggle. 'Leave me alone,' she cried, pushing him as
best she could.

'Oh, so we like a tussle, do we?' Ruddy's eyes gleamed and he threw her onto the bed.

'Please, leave me alone. I never wanted anything like this to happen,' Gabriella remonstrated, trying to move out of his hold.

'Oh, come on, Gabriella. I know you're young, but don't let's play games, darling. You've been hot for this ever since I arrived. I've seen the way you and your husband behave with one another. I'll bet he rarely comes near you. Anyway, it's a known fact that Ricardo lays that Mexican tornado Ambrosia. He's not likely to give up a hot little number like that just because he married a schoolgirl. Now, come on, baby—let me teach you to enjoy yourself in bed. I'll bet he hasn't.'

Gabriella felt a rush of unprecedented anger grip her. And with it came a wave of unexpected strength. She raised her leg and gave Rudy a hard blow with her knee that sent him reeling back on the floor.

'You little bitch,' he muttered, grimacing. 'You're nothing but a tease.'

'I'm leaving,' Gabriella threw, getting up and hurrying into the living room.

'Oh, yes? And how exactly do you plan to do that?'

'I'll take a taxi back to the castle.'

'Really? Well, good luck to you. There's a festival on,' he said with satisfaction. 'All the taxis will be busy.' Gabriella felt a sudden rush of panic, but Ruddy shook his head ruefully. 'Look, don't worry. I'm sorry if I frightened you. Maybe I should have gone about this more tactfully. Let's forget about the whole thing and stay friends, okay? I'm sorry. Really.' He moved towards her, stretched out his hand and smiled disarmingly. 'I got it wrong. I'm sorry. I'll take you home now if you like, and we'll say no more about it.'

Gabriella hesitated again. She had no desire to go to the end of the street with this man, and wished she'd done as Ricardo had said and left with him to go back to Maldoravia. But it was too late for regrets. Now all she wanted was to return to the safety of the castle.

'All right,' she agreed reluctantly. 'Are you sure it's not dangerous to ride in this weather?' She glanced out of the window, to where heavy raindrops were beginning to fall.

'Oh, Lord, of course not. We're experienced riders. You're not scared, are you?' he teased, his eyes meeting hers in a daring challenge.

'Of course I'm not scared,' she scoffed, tossing her head back. She would not for a moment show any anxiety.

Back on the bike, they headed back on the road they'd travelled. To her horror, the bike picked up speed.

'Not so fast,' she shouted above the wind as a wave of nervousness overtook her.

But Ruddy just laughed, stepped on the gas and whizzed around the corners of the small country road at breakneck speed, forcing her to cling to him for dear life. In the back of her mind a niggling picture of Ricardo looking thoroughly disapproving haunted her. Oh, how she wished she had listened to him, and that he were here right now.

Another sharp turn had her screaming with fear. Then suddenly she heard the loud blare of a horn. The bike screeched, then swerved off the road, and she was flying through the air.

After that there was darkness.

*   *   *

Ricardo had not returned to Maldoravia, as he had led them to believe, but had merely driven to Salzburg for a morning of meetings. When he returned to the *schloss* at lunchtime he was met by his sister.

'So there you are. Hans told me you had decided to stay. Why did you go to Salzburg so early?'

'I had a meeting with a friend of mine from the music festival. I'm a patron. We had breakfast at the Sacher. Is my wife home yet?'

'No, of course not. They only left about an hour and a half ago. I think they are going to lunch at a *heurigen*.'

'I see.' Ricardo looked stern. 'I don't approve of her going off with the likes of Ruddy Hofstetten. I don't like him.'

'Why on earth not? He seems a perfectly nice young man to me. And Jamie's an absolute hoot. He tells such funny stories. I haven't laughed like this in years.'

'I've heard some rather disagreeable stories about Ruddy and his pals,' Ricardo continued as they stepped into the drawing room. 'I don't like the idea of my wife being alone with him.'

'Well, she's not alone with him,' Constanza pointed out in a matter-of-fact tone. 'Jamie is with them.'

'Hmm.' Somehow he could not rid himself of the uneasy feeling that had haunted him all morning that all was not right. 'Where did they go?' he enquired, accepting a glass of champagne from his sister.

'I don't know, exactly. But why are you so worried? Gabriella seems to be having fun.'

'That isn't the point.'

'Really, Ricardo, you're acting like a jealous husband, for goodness' sake.'

'That's ridiculous,' he retorted. 'I'm merely concerned about her being out in this weather with two reckless young men.'

'God, you sound like her father, not her husband.' Constanza gave him a look that spoke volumes but said nothing more. Perhaps he needed to come to the conclusion that he was far more taken with his young wife than he himself realised. If that was the case then she was happy. The more she knew Gabriella, the more she liked her. She just hoped that the two would work themselves out in the end.

It was four in the afternoon when a police car drove up to the Schloss and two solid-looking officers dressed in green marched up the steps. Hans opened the heavy front door. Moments later he was knocking anxiously on the door of the den, where Constanza, Wilhelm and Ricardo were watching a tennis match on TV.

'Your Highness, you are wanted in the hall,' he said, addressing Ricardo, his expression worried.

'What? Who on earth would want Ricardo?' Constanza exclaimed, her face tilting upwards in surprise.

'I'm afraid it is not good news,' Hans said, shaking his white head.

'Gabriella.' Ricardo was already out of his chair and marching into the hall, where he nodded to the two officers. 'What is going on?' he asked, in a voice that rang with authority.

'I'm afraid it is your wife, Your Highness.'

'What about her?'

'There has been an accident.'

'An accident?' Ricardo paled, clenched his fingers tight and forced himself to remain calm.

'Oh, my God!' Constanza exclaimed anxiously, following him out of the room with her husband.

'Where is she?' Wilhelm asked.

'The helicopter flew her to Salzburg, Herr Graf. We know no more than that.'

'What about the drivers of the bikes?' Wilhelm asked.

'There was only one, sir. He was not badly hurt. They kept him in the nearby village hospital to check him out. The more seriously injured was Her Royal Highness.'

'We must go at once,' Ricardo said, tight-lipped. 'Wilhelm, get a chopper.'

'In this weather? Forget it. I'll drive you. It'll be quicker.'

'Wait for me,' Constanza cried, grabbing a couple of old Loden jackets lying on one of the hall chairs. 'Thank you, Officer,' she said to the policeman, then rushed out of the front door to jump into the back of the Range Rover that Wilhelm was already revving up.

'You're all right now.' She heard a soft voice close by as she came to.

'Where am I?' Gabriella whispered, opening her eyes, a dizzy feeling making her close them again immediately.

'You are in hospital in Salzburg. You had a motorbike accident and suffered a mild concussion. You also broke your arm. It was thought preferable to bring you here.'

'Oh.' She closed her eyes again, the scenes of earlier that afternoon playing out before her. All at once a rush of tears burned her eyes and she wished, oh, how she wished that she had listened to Ricardo, and had not let her pride dictate her actions. But it was too late for that. Ricardo would be furious when he found out what had happened. Now, instead of getting better, things would probably get worse between them.

'Are you all right, my child?' The soft voice spoke again and she opened her eyes to see a smiling face under a wimple. 'I am Sister Perpetua,' the nun told her, pressing a gentle hand on hers. 'There is no need for you to be unhappy or frightened any longer. All is well, and you will be fine in a few days.'

'Does—does anyone know I'm here?' Gabriella asked in a small voice.

'Yes. A message has been sent to your sister-in-law, Grafin Wiesthun. Apparently the young man with whom you were riding provided the police with the address. I imagine your family will be here soon.'

Gabriella nodded and swallowed.

'The other good news,' the nun said, beaming, 'is that the baby is all right.'

'The baby?' Gabriela looked at her blankly.

'Yes, my dear. Your baby.'

'My baby? But—'

'You mean you didn't know that you were pregnant?' the English nun asked kindly.

'No! I… That is, I had no idea. How could this have

happened?' she whispered, trying to draw herself up
in the bed, wondering if she was going mad.

'In the usual manner, I imagine,' the nun replied
with a touch of wry humour. 'You are a married
woman, I gather, so it is to be expected.'

'I didn't think that—I just thought my period was
late,' Gabriella mumbled, almost to herself. 'It never
occurred to me that… Oh, my God,' she whispered as
the implications of what she had just been told sank
in. 'Sister, please, do not tell anyone.' She turned in
panic to the nun and clasped her hand with her
good one.

'But why not? Surely your husband will want to
know that the child is all right.'

'He doesn't know yet and I—well, there are reasons
why I would rather tell him myself,' she said, a dull
flush covering her cheeks.

'Well, of course, my child. It is for you to break the
good news. I will tell Dr Braun not to mention it either.'

'Oh, please. This is such a surprise. It will he for
him too, you see,' she added quickly.

'A happy one, I hope?' The nun looked straight into
her eyes, read the confusion there and squeezed her
hand.

'I—yes. That is, I don't really know.' Gabriella
swallowed the growing knot in her throat.

'Are you not happily married?'

'Yes. No. That is… I must sound so stupid. But the
truth is I don't know anything any more. Everything
is so confused and mixed up.' Her hand trembled in
Sister Perpetua's.

At that moment a knock on the door interrupted her confidences.

'Ah. This must be your sister-in-law now,' the nun said, rising from the chair and giving Gabriella's hand a last squeeze. 'We'll talk later. Now, don't get too tired,' she said, moving across the room to open the door.

But instead of Constanza it was Ricardo who stood in the doorway and then made his way quickly across the room.

'Gabriella,' he said, looking down at her and taking her hand in his.

'Ricardo. What are you doing here?'

'I could ask you the same thing,' he said, looking down at her, his expression stern.

'I…I'm so sorry. You were right. I shouldn't have gone.' Again a rush of tears surfaced that she could do nothing to stop.

But instead of showing anger, Ricardo's face changed immediately. He sat on the edge of the bed and stroked her hair gently, then dropped a kiss on her brow. 'Oh, Gabriella, darling, did you think I would be angry with you?' he murmured, a smile hovering about his lips. 'I'm just thrilled to know that you are all right and that nothing worse happened. I can't wait to get my hands on that little skunk Hofstetten. The police report says he was driving far too fast and that the fault of the accident was entirely his.'

He ground his teeth and Gabriella felt the pressure on her hand increase. It was wonderful to feel him so close, to feel the pressure of his fingers on hers. Even in her diminished state she could sense that same familiar tingle course through her, and she let out a sigh. God only knew what he would do if he knew what had happened at that inn, she reflected.

'Now, you must stay quietly here for a few days and rest,' Ricardo said, pinching her chin and smiling down at her.

'But can't I leave? Go back to the *schloss*?'

'Not for a couple of days.'

'Oh, but please, Ricardo, I don't want to stay here on my own. Please ask them if I can go back. I'm sure they'll let me.'

Gabriella tried to put the other thing out of her mind. She would think about it in a few days—once she was better. She would have to think what to do. On the one hand she experienced a sensation of wonder. On the other she realised in a quick moment of clarity that once he knew she was carrying his child Ricardo might insist she stay with him. It was all so complicated, so difficult. How she wished that he really loved her and that she could confide in him. But the way he was being now was just because of the accident. Soon he would be off again, to the arms of Ambrosia, or to some other sophisticated worldly woman's bed.

'Darling!' Constanza burst into the room, interrupting her inner thoughts, her arms overflowing with boxes of Mozart Kugelen—traditional Salzburg chocolates filled with marzipan—and flowers. 'I'm sorry you had an accident. I'm furious with Ruddy. I heard it was all his fault. Which just goes to prove that Ricardo was right about him after all.'

'What did you say about him?' Gabriella asked uneasily.

'That I think he's a bad character and that I've heard a few wild tales of his behaviour.'

'Ah.'

Ricardo looked at her closely, his brows meeting over the ridge of his nose as they were prone to do when he was concentrating. Had something happened? he wondered. Gabriella looked pale. But that was natural in her present condition. Or was there something more—something she didn't want to tell him?

For the moment he wouldn't press her, he decided, as Wilhelm joined them in the room and came over to talk to Gabriella.

In the end they let her leave the next day, under strict orders not to overdo it and to stay in bed for a few days.

'That's odd,' Constanza remarked, 'usually nowadays they try and get you up and about in no time.'

'Mmm.' Gabriella made a non-committal sound as the Range Rover, driven by Ricardo, entered the castle gates and they drove up to the front steps, where Wilhelm awaited them.

'Gabriella, how good to have you back among us,' Wilhelm exclaimed, helping her to alight.

Ricardo watched her. She still looked very pale, and it was obvious that the accident had affected her more deeply than he'd at first suspected. Was there anything else upsetting her? he wondered, remembering his pithy encounter with Ruddy Hofstetten the day before. Ruddy had returned to the castle sheepishly, to pick up his things, but had not escaped a lashing from Ricardo's tongue.

'If I ever find out that you molested my wife in any way you will have me to deal with,' he'd thrown bitingly. 'It's bad enough that you almost killed her. I advise you to keep away from her, or things will go badly for you.'

'Are you threatening me?' Ruddy had bristled.

'I'm warning you. I don't want to see your face anywhere near her.'

Ruddy had drawn himself up, about to retort, then thought better of it. Ricardo did not look like a man to mess with and, frankly, the idea of seducing Gabriella had grown old after the events of the past few days. Better to move on to pastures new, he'd figured with a shrug.

'You don't have to worry about me,' he'd said with a little laugh. 'You're welcome to your schoolgirl wife. I like them more sophisticated myself. A bit more bedroom knowledge needed for my taste.'

A few seconds later he had been nursing his jaw on the floor of Wilhelm's library. He had departed within the hour.

But now, as he observed his wife's pallor, Ricardo wished he'd done him more damage. Somehow he could not get it out of his head that Ruddy had in some manner upset her. Oh, well, it was too late to go over that territory again, and the sooner he got her home the better. But rest she must, and he would see to it that she did—despite her protests to the contrary.

*   *   *

Once she was installed in her large bed Gabriella was finally left alone and could think. For the past forty-eight hours she had done nothing but reflect upon her present situation and all its implications.

A baby. A baby that would grow up into a child. Ricardo's child.

She swallowed and fingered the edge of the sheet nervously. What was she to do? If she told him the truth then that would be it. He would expect her to remain married to him. She would be shackled for life. Or a good number of years anyway. If only things were different between them—if she knew that he loved her it would be different. But she was certain that although he was fond of her, enjoyed taking her to his bed, he was not in love with her. His sense of duty was what drove him to be so kind and nice to her. And every time she allowed herself to believe that perhaps his feelings were more engaged than she'd thought, she recalled that image of him and Ambrosia, side by side on the forward deck of the yacht, the intimacy between them so palpable, so impossible to deny.

She didn't want to be like other royal couples she could think of, with a third party in her marriage. If there was another woman in his life, then better that he live with her, not pretend that all was well with his marriage when all it would cause was unhappiness for everyone. Right now he was being charming—refusing to leave for Maldoravia until she was completely well, spending time with her while she rested. They had even played cards together and laughed at a TV programme. Then last night when he'd come to bed he had leaned over and kissed her so tenderly that she'd nearly collapsed with pain and wanting. He'd taken her into his arms and kissed her gently, prying her lips open and causing such new and deep sensations to ripple through her that she hadn't been able to help submitting to his caresses.

Now she closed her eyes and remembered the way he'd stroked her breasts, the way his lips had followed where his hands had left off, how she'd cried with unmitigated delight when he'd brought her to completion then entered her, delving deep inside her being, far deeper into her heart and soul than she could have imagined possible.

Gabriella let out a ragged sigh. She felt trapped. Trapped by her own feelings and the impossibility of her situation. She had to face the truth—that she was in love with her husband and that he, although he treated her with the utmost respect and kindness, was doing no more than his duty in the completion of a promise to a dying man.

She had to get away—had to leave him now before it was too late and they were both caught for ever in a web that was not of their making. She couldn't bear to live like this, to have him make love to her knowing that he was probably going to another woman. She would never know a moment's peace or respite. Her life would turn into a living hell where she saw potential threat in every other woman. No. That was no way to live. She'd seen that movie once too often— friends of her father's, whose wives had given them all they wanted but had maintained several mistresses in tow, some who even appeared socially and had to be tolerated. That was not how she planned to live her life. Whatever it cost her, and however much it hurt, she would make the break now.

But what about the baby?

Her hand slipped to her stomach and she closed her eyes. Was it really possible that from their few incidences of lovemaking this could happen? She had talked to the doctor and apparently there was no doubt about her pregnancy. That was why she had to rest longer than normally would have been required, must make sure nothing could harm the tiny speck of life growing within her. But what a responsibility it was to think of beginning a new life, just she and her child.

She would wait for a few days before taking her final decision. She would do nothing until she was entirely well again—until she felt stable and strong enough to make the right decision and stick with it.

It was only a day trip to London, with a business lunch at Harry's Bar, then back on the royal plane to Salzburg. But Ricardo worried that Gabriella didn't seem to be looking any better. In fact, since her return to Constanza's home she seemed more tired, and looked paler still. He thought she had lost weight.

As the plane flew over the Channel to London he thought about the night before last, when he'd held her in his arms and she'd opened to him, about how he was experiencing new and wonderful feelings that he had not experienced with any other woman. It was crazy that at his age and after all the women he'd bedded his wife should turn out to be so very special, should have that certain something he'd been looking for all these years.

When she was better he would take her away for that honeymoon they'd never had, he resolved, a smile hovering about his lips as they flew over Windsor Castle and headed for City Airport.

It was raining hard as he headed towards the entrance of the terminal, where his car awaited him, and he was walking quickly through the milling throng when he saw a face he recognised.

Ambrosia saw him, handsome and tanned in a light grey suit, taking purposeful strides towards the main entrance. She lifted a manicured hand and waved, calling his name. He stopped, turned, and, smiling, moved to where she stood.

'Hello, Ambro. How are you?'

'Oh, fine. All the better for seeing you,' she responded archly.

'Are you going into London? Can I give you a lift?'

Ambrosia took a snap decision to dismiss the vehicle that had been hired to meet her. 'Actually, that would be lovely,' she murmured, linking her arm in his. 'How long do you plan to be here?'

'Oh, not very long. I go back to Salzburg tonight unless this meeting prolongs itself. Then I may have to stay over.'

'Where's the meeting?'

'At the bank with Ludo. A loan Maldoravia wants approved for a new drain system throughout the country.'

'I didn't know Ludo was back in town,' Ambrosia said thoughtfully, her mind working furiously. If she could get Ricardo's meeting prolonged, then that would open up any number of possibilities. For Ambrosia was convinced that if she could get him alone for a single evening all would go back to the way it had been.

As she seated herself elegantly in the vehicle she smiled at him, a steely determination taking hold of her. She would not let this man escape—would not allow a child barely out of the schoolroom to displace her in this man's bed and affections. Ricardo had brought too much into her life for that. She had never hoped for marriage, knew that was impossible. But she was damned if anything as trivial as his nuptials would change their lives.

When he dropped her off in Chelsea, she smiled regretfully. 'If by any chance you do stay over, promise me that we can have dinner together. I miss you, Ricky. After all, we were good friends as well as lovers, weren't we?'

'Of course.'

'So we should see more of one another. You haven't been anywhere near me for the past couple of months, and that hurts.' She could be very convincing when she wanted. In a quick feminine gesture she leaned forward and straightened his already straight tie, then lifted her face and touched his lips with hers. It was fleeting and affectionate. Then she looped her large Hermès bag on her arm and exited the vehicle, leaving a lingering whiff of Calèche in her wake.

As soon as the car drove off, and before the door could be answered by the maid, she was on her cellphone. 'Ludo—is that you?'

'Oh, hello, Ambro. What can I do for you?'

'Something terribly important. I just drove in from the airport with Ricardo. He's on his way to his meeting with you at the bank right now.'

'Yes, and…?'

'And I want you to make things drag on long enough so that he has to spend the night here in town. Make some excuse. Invent something. Be creative.'

'Good Lord. Not up to your tricks again, are you, Ambro?'

'No, just consolidating my position—which has been a bit risky of late.'

'Well, I suppose I could do that for an old friend.'

'You're sure it'll work out?'

'Of course. Trust me, baby. Ricky's very keen on this new drainage system he wants installed in the Principality. I'll find a way of making him stay over.'

'Good. Just make sure you do, okay?'

'Fine. I'll give you the position later on in the day.'

'Thank you, Ludo. You're an absolute darling.'

'Any time, gorgeous, any time.'

CHAPTER TEN

'I REALLY don't understand why you have to have those other documents right away,' Ricardo said, frowning. It was five o'clock. Even though it was summer, he didn't want to fly out too late.

'Look, I'm sorry, old chap,' Ludo said apologetically. 'It's these damn new EU regulations. Why don't you stay the night? I'll have all the papers faxed in by tomorrow morning, and we can go over them and sign then.'

'I really wanted to get back to my wife,' Ricardo said reluctantly. 'But I suppose there's nothing for it but to do that.'

'Mmm.' Ludo, a good-looking chestnut-haired man in his mid-thirties, eyed him carefully. 'How about dinner tonight?'

'Why not? I've nothing else on the agenda. What shall we say? Eight-thirty at Mark's?'

'Sounds good to me,' Ludo replied, raising his palms and getting up. 'See you later, old chap.'

Ricardo followed suit. 'Yes. See you later.'

The Rolls drove him to Cadogan Square, where he owned a house fully staffed all year round. A secretary had phoned from Ludo's office, so he was expected. It was almost six o'clock. Ricardo went upstairs into a large suite of rooms and was preparing to take a shower when his cellphone rang.

'Hello?'

'Hello. It's me—Ambrosia. Are you on your way home?'

'Actually, no. I'm spending the night here in London.'

'Really? Well, then, you'd better stay true to your promise.'

'What was that?' He frowned abstractedly and pulled off his tie.

'We agreed that if you stayed in town you'd take me to dinner—remember?'

'Damn, *cara*, you're right. I forgot. It was an unexpected last-minute decision. I've made dinner arrangements with Ludo, but I suppose there is no reason why you shouldn't join us. We've dealt with business for the day.'

'I'd love to. Where and when?'

'I'll come round and pick you up a little before eight, if that suits you?'

'Fine. See you then.'

And it did suit her. Ambrosia hung up, rubbing her hands with glee. Finally chance had played into her hands. And she had Ludo to thank, she reminded herself. She owed him one. He had acted brilliantly. And now the evening was set up in such a way that she would recover her former lover with no problem.

What was keeping him? Gabriella wondered as she sat in the sitting room waiting for Constanza and Wilhelm to appear for drinks. It was after seven o'clock—six in England—and there was still no sign of Ricardo. Just as she was beginning to worry her cellphone rang.

'Hello?'

'Gabriella, *cara mia*.'

She swallowed at the endearment. 'Hello. How was your day?'

'Fine. Except we didn't finish all the business we had planned, and I'm going to have to stay the night and come home tomorrow afternoon, I'm afraid.'

'Oh.' She felt a wave of disappointment engulf her, but pulled herself together. 'Well, that's fine.'

'I'm sorry, but this is such an important project for Maldoravia—I can't let it flounder.'

'Of course not. Everything's fine here,' she lied, wishing she could forget the morning sickness that had overtaken her that day, and all that it signified.

'Good. Then I'll see you tomorrow afternoon. You are feeling better, aren't you?'

'Oh, yes, I'm doing much better.'

'Good. Then sleep well, *cara mia*, and see you tomorrow.'

'Goodnight,' she whispered, letting out a shaky sigh and wishing that she didn't have to lie to him the whole time, that everything could be easy and straightforward and simple.

Which it wasn't.

'I do adore this egg with caviar,' Ambrosia cooed as they sat at Mark's, ensconced together at their table. The head waiter had just told them that Ludo had sent a message saying he would be running rather late and to begin dinner without him.

'Typical,' Ricardo said, shaking his head and admiring Ambrosia's perfect profile and the ruby and diamond earrings she was wearing. They were Cartier. He knew. He'd given them to her not that long ago.

'So, tell me, Ricky darling, how is wedded life suiting you?' she said, turning slightly and smiling, all understanding and interest.

'Well, it's not as simple as I thought it would be. Gabriella is young and needs help finding her feet. Also she had an accident. She's recovering at my sister's in Austria.'

'Poor child,' she murmured. 'What happened?'

'Oh, nothing much. She fell off a motorbike.'

'A motorbike?' Ambrosia raised her perfectly plucked eyebrows in mock surprise. 'Why, I never thought you'd allow your wife to go out on a motorbike, Ricky darling. I'm most surprised.'

'Well, actually, I didn't. I wasn't there.'

'Then who was the driver?'

'Ruddy Hofstetten,' he said reluctantly.

'You don't say?' Ambrosia leaned back against the sofa and watched him thoughtfully. He was scowling. Something must definitely have been going on between Gabriella and young Hofstetten for him to look so glum. Wouldn't that be a perfect piece of gossip for the scandalmongers? she reflected, wondering how she could use it to her advantage. 'Is she all right after the fall?' she asked, assuming an expression of deep concern.

'Yes. Yes, she is. Though she seems to be taking longer to get well than I thought she would. She looks pale and is rather tired.'

'Poor girl,' she said in a sympathetic voice. 'It can't be much fun for you, I imagine?'

'No. I worry about her. It's weird. A few months ago I was free as a bird, and now I seem to have all these responsibilities.'

'Well, you chose them, darling,' she said, letting her fingers slip over his and squeezing his hand. 'But why don't you forget about all that for tonight and we can enjoy ourselves? Let's go to Annabel's afterwards and dance. I love dancing with you, Ricky. I miss it. In fact, I miss a lot of things that we used to do rather well together,' she purred, lifting her glass by the stem and raising it conspiratorially.

Ricardo smiled and his eyes twinkled. 'We did have good times together, Ambro, didn't we?'

'Did?' She arched a brow and smiled suggestively.

'Well, I'm a married man now.'

'What has that got to do with anything?' she insisted, meeting his eyes full on. 'You know I knew you'd never marry me, Ricky, that one day this would have to happen. After all, you need a son and heir. But I never thought it would affect our relationship in the bigger scheme of things.'

'That's very broad-minded of you, Ambro,' he said, twirling his glass and looking at his watch. 'I wonder where Ludo has got to?'

'Oh, he's probably been held up. But, darling—about us. We're not children. You and I have been around the block a few times. We know the name of the game. Now, why don't we stop pretending that you and I are *passé* and have a relaxing night to catch up? On second thoughts, I think I'd rather go straight home than out dancing.' She let her other hand slide under the table and onto his thigh, feeling the tension in his muscles. Surreptitiously she glanced at her watch. Jerry, the tabloid photographer she often gave tips to, and whom she'd phoned earlier in the evening, must be ready outside, waiting for their exit. 'I think we should just sign the bill and go,' she murmured.

'Okay. One drink at your place, then I must be off home.' He smiled at her and beckoned the waiter.

'Of course. I'll dash to the loo and meet you in the hall.'

'Fine.'

Several minutes later they were exiting the club. The Rolls drew up and Ambrosia took Ricky's arm. 'Look,' she said bringing her face close to his. 'Look how lovely the moon is tonight. It reminds me of that song—remember?—the one we always used to listen to in Sardinia?'

'I remember.' He turned and looked down at her. At that moment she raised her lips to his, planting a quick kiss there and praying that Jerry had got the shot. She hadn't seen any flashbulbs, but then she'd told him to be ultra-discreet.

Ten minutes later they were driving up to the Chelsea townhouse where Ambrosia lived. On the steps she took her key out and giggled. 'Just like old times, isn't it? What have you done with all your security? I didn't see them about.'

'They're here somewhere, I suppose. Just being discreet—thank God.'

'Well, don't let's dawdle here,' she said, pulling him inside. 'God, it's good to have you back here, Ricky. The place hasn't been the same without you.'

She slipped her arms around his neck and drew him towards her.

'Ambro, I said a drink, for old time's sake, and I meant it,' he said, disengaging himself.

'Oh, pooh—don't be so priggish. What man doesn't have a mistress, I ask you?'

'That's not the point. I feel responsible towards Gabriella. We're just beginning to get our relationship on its feet.'

'Well, she's hardly going to imagine you're here with me, is she?' she argued reasonably.

'No. But that doesn't make it any better.'

'You know, I never imagined you as a goody-goody,' she exclaimed, annoyed at his reluctance. 'What on earth can it matter that you're here and that we're going to make love?'

'We are not going to make love, Ambro. I thought I'd made that quite plain.'

'She's only your wife, for God's sake. Can't you get her pregnant? That way she'll be busy with her babies and won't bother us.'

'Life isn't quite as simple as that,' he murmured, distancing himself and moving towards the fireplace. 'There's more to marriage than I had imagined.'

Ambrosia watched him, taken aback. This wasn't going quite as she had planned.

'Well, forget it. Just for tonight. A goodbye send-off, if you will,' she purred, moving next to him and drawing his mouth down to hers. But Ricardo moved firmly away.

'I said no, Ambro, and I meant it. And now I really must be off.'

Red anger blinded her. It was too humiliating for words, too lowering for her to bear. He had come here, kissed her, and then, almost as if he were bored, had looked at his watch and said he had to go home. She would not forgive him lightly.

After he left Ambrosia stood with her back against the closed front door, nursing her fury. She hadn't had Jerry take pictures for any specific reason—more as a safeguard for the future. But now as her anger seethed she knew exactly what she would do. Marching to the telephone, she dialled.

'Jerry? Hi. Did you get the shots?'

'Beauts, darlin', real beauts. Got the kiss and the works. Boy, these will sell for a bloody fortune.'

'Well, I'm glad to hear you say that,' she replied, her voice laced with venom, 'because I'd like you to sell them with a story, to as many tabloids as you can get your busy little hands on.'

'Really, love? When?'

'How about right now? Come over and I'll write up the text for you. If we're quick we may just make tomorrow's papers.'

'You got it, babe. I'll be there in twenty.'

'Perfect, Jerry. I'll be waiting.'

The next morning dawned rainy again, and Gabriella glanced out of the window, wishing she could see a few palms, sun and sea. Then, as she was about to turn around and have another sleep, a sudden rush of nausea had her stumbling to the bathroom. Oh, God. How long would this last? It made her feel so terrible.

After half an hour she lay back in bed and decided

to ask for breakfast here in her room rather than go down. Constanza was going into town this morning early—had probably already left with the children—and Wilhelm was in Munich. The weird thing was, she realised, after calling downstairs and giving instructions, after the nausea passed she felt positively hungry.

Several minutes later a knock on the door announced the maid, carrying a large tray with the breakfast and the papers. The girl, Inge, smiled and said, *'Guten morgen.'* She spoke no English, so communication was limited.

Once the tray was safely installed on her knees and Inge had disappeared, Gabriella poured herself a cup of coffee before drinking her orange juice. There were several papers, and she placed them beside her on the bed. The family bought English papers—Constanza said she loved the gossip that came in many of them.

After eating a piece of toast and a boiled egg, Gabriella settled in for a comfortable morning relaxing and reading while sipping her coffee. She flipped over the papers and picked up the first one, then paled as she saw the picture splashed on the front page and the headlines.

'Oh, my God,' she whispered, her eyes filling with angry tears as she read, unbelieving, the words above a picture of a woman and a man whom she recognised only too well kissing in the moonlight.

Moonlight Escapade for Just-Wed Prince, the headline read. But worse was to come when she read the text, for in it were details—not all correct—of her biking accident. It even mentioned Ruddy, and implied that she was having an affair with him. How could this be? Who could have done this? And there was Ricardo, on the front page of the paper, kissing Ambrosia for all the world to see.

All her worst nightmares had become reality, Gabriella realised, her hands trembling as she discovered more pictures inside, and in another publication. All her fears were well-founded. Thank God she hadn't told him about the baby—hadn't risked her future with this man who was proving to be all she'd expected. The dream that one day they might have a real marriage had been nothing but that: a dream.

Pushing away the tray and pulling back the bedclothes, Gabriella got up. She ran into the bathroom, tears of anger pouring down her cheeks. But she was determined to be in control.

And out of here before he returned.

With this goal in mind she quickly entered the shower. Twenty minutes later she was dressed and packed. And ready to make a new life away from Prince Ricardo of Maldoravia, whom she hoped she'd never set eyes on again.

CHAPTER ELEVEN

'LEFT? You mean she's gone?' Ricardo exclaimed, staring at Hans the butler in shock. 'But when—and where to?'

'I'm afraid Her Royal Highness didn't say where she was going, sir. I heard the instructions to the hire chauffeur, of course, which were to take her to the airport in Munich.' Hans hesitated, then said in a softer tone, 'She seemed somewhat agitated, sir, if I may say so. I had the impression…'

'Go on,' Ricardo urged. 'What impression?'

'That all was not right,' he murmured, looking down.

'What gave you that impression?'

'Well, sir, without meaning to be indiscreet, the maid Inge found several newspapers strewn around the bedroom…' He paused.

'Yes? And?'

'Well, there was a picture of you, sir. With a lady.'

'Oh, my God. So that's what the press were trying to get in touch with me about this morning. I paid no attention—thought it was unimportant—had the secretary deal with… Hans, get me those papers immediately.'

'Very well, sir. I think the Grafin has them in the drawing room.'

'Then I shall go there at once. Thanks,' he added, moving towards the door and opening it.

Constanza sat by the window. She looked at him and shook her head. 'Really, Ricky, I can't believe that you're making such a muck of things. I tried to stop Gabriella leaving,' she continued, getting up in her agitation, 'but she refused to listen. And after I saw the front pages of those tabloids, frankly I'm not surprised—and I don't blame her one iota.'

'Show me.' His face was hard as granite.

'You mean you haven't seen them?'

'Constanza, I read the *Financial Times*, not the bloody tabloids,' he threw at her.

'Well, if this is how you plan to behave, then perhaps you should change your reading matter,' she responded tartly, thrusting a newspaper at him.

'Oh, Lord. I don't believe it,' he muttered, unfolding the paper and staring at himself kissing Ambrosia under a full moon. 'That bitch. I can't believe she would do this to me.'

'Well, you know what they say about a woman scorned. It was very foolish of you to go out with her at all. Unless...' Constanza paused and looked at him speculatively. 'Did you give her some bad news?'

'I suppose in a way I did. I told her that I was sticking to my decision, that it really was over between us and that I didn't like being set up and wouldn't be staying the night. You see, Con, although this marriage of mine has happened in such a strange manner, I have...deep feelings for Gabriella. I—' He cut himself off and looked out of the window, his features harsh in the afternoon light. 'I don't want to lose her, and she plans to separate from me in a couple of months.'

'What?'

'Yes.' He dropped the paper on the table and flopped into an armchair, dragging his fingers through his hair. 'It's a long story. But by Maldoravian law if we want a divorce we have to stay married for a minimum of six months. Then a separation of two years is necessary before we can petition for divorce.'

'A divorce?' Constanza cried, shaking her head. 'But what nonsense is this? Anyone can see that you are deeply attracted to one another.'

'I believe so,' he said with the ghost of a smile. 'Unfortunately, this is not the first time that Ambrosia has come between us. You see, she had no illusions about marrying me, but she believed that after my wedding things would simply continue as they always had done. Frankly, I thought so too. But then—'

'But then?' Constanza prodded more gently.

'But then I discovered that I really didn't want any other woman than Gabriella.'

'Well, why on earth didn't you tell her so?'

'I was going to. I just didn't feel the time was right. Perhaps I wasn't entirely certain myself,' he muttered, picking the paper off the coffee table again. 'The important thing now is to find her. I can't have her gallivanting all over the world by herself. Plus, she's not well. I suppose she managed to leave without security noticing?' he added bitterly. 'I really must do something about those agents. This is the second time she's slipped through my fingers.'

'What I'm most worried about,' Constanza said,

looking her brother in the eye, 'is that she still doesn't seem to have totally recovered from that accident. She looks pale and not herself. Oh, God, where can she have gone?'

'I don't know.' He dragged his fingers through his hair again and got up, starting to pace the room. 'Brazil, perhaps. Though something tells me that she wouldn't go home again so soon. I really can't think.' He threw up his hands, then dropped them. 'We'd better start by trying the airport.'

'Princess, how do you feel about seeing your husband kissing another woman on the front page of this morning's paper?'

As she made her way through the international departure terminal Gabriella was assailed by reporters. Who could have told them she would be here? she wondered, pulling on her shades angrily. This was all she needed. And where was she going? She didn't even know. She'd simply packed and left, planning to buy a ticket to somewhere here at the airport. But that was impossible now. The whole world would know where she was. For the first time she regretted not having the bodyguards who kept this kind of thing at bay.

Hastily she changed course and, waving to the chauffeur of the hire car, hurried back towards it and climbed quickly in before the press could catch her. But even as the car moved away from the kerb flash-bulbs popped and faces were plastered to the darkened windows of the large Mercedes.

Finally the vehicle left the airport and they were back on the highway.

'Where do you wish to go?' the driver asked, masking his curiosity behind a poker face.

'Go? I…' She hesitated a moment, then made a snap decision. She would go to Switzerland—go to Madame Delorme, her old headmistress. At least there she could hide without anyone knowing where she was.

'I need you to drive to Lausanne, in Switzerland,' she said at last.

'Very well, *madame*. It will take several hours.'

'I don't care,' she replied, sinking into the deep leather seat and closing her eyes.

Anywhere was better than here.

'There's no trace of her,' Ricardo exclaimed several hours later.

'Come and see the TV. Look.' Wilhelm pointed at the screen. 'There she is at Munich airport, but then she's getting back in the car.'

'We'd better trace it at once. God, this is awful,' Ricardo murmured, clenching his fists. 'I hate to think of what she must be going through—what she must be thinking.'

'The worst,' Wilhelm said unsympathetically.

'Yes. I should think the last person on the planet she wants to see right now is you,' Constanza added helpfully.

'I'm very well aware of that,' Ricardo responded through gritted teeth. 'I just want to know—number one, where she is, and number two, how to make her listen to me.'

'Both of which may be difficult under the circumstances,' Constanza murmured, eyeing her brother carefully. He looked determined and furious, with that same cold anger that she remembered in their father. But behind the angry front she read worry and concern.

'Have you tried her mobile?' she said at last.

'Only about fifty million times.'

'Right. Well, in the meantime we'd better have a drink,' Wilhelm said in a more practical tone, moving over to the drinks tray. He poured Ricardo a stiff whisky and handed it to him. 'Don't worry, old chap, we'll find her soon.'

It felt strange to be back at the school which she had left only months ago, graduating with honours. So much had occurred in her life since then—so many changes that it felt like a lifetime ago.

'It is wonderful to see you again,' said Madame Delorme, an elderly slim woman with grey hair swept back into a severe chignon, welcoming Gabriella warmly into her office. 'What *bon vent* brings you here? Are you staying a while, or merely passing through?'

'Uh, actually I thought I might stay a little.' Gabriella fiddled with her handbag, not knowing where to begin. It was all very difficult.

'Well, let's sit down and have a cup of tea,' Madame Delorme replied smoothly. Her eyes swept over her old pupil and she frowned inwardly. All was not well with Gabriella, that was clear as day. She looked pale, and too thin. And also she who had always shone among the crowd seemed tired and almost forlorn, as though all the spark had been punched out of her.

Tactfully Madame said nothing, but allowed Gabriella to relax. She told her of school doings, news she'd received from some of the old girls who had been classmates of Gabriella and who she might not be in touch with.

'In fact,' she said, glancing up and nodding to the maid as a tea tray was set down, 'I was quite surprised that you didn't invite Cynthia and Agnes to the wedding. They were your best friends. You are still in touch, I hope?'

'Uh, yes. We e-mail each other. But unfortunately my wedding was planned in such a rush that there was no time to invite anyone. If there had been you would have been on my guest list. You know that, Madame,' she said, with a ghost of her old mischievous smile dawning.

'I know I would,' the headmistress said, smiling at her warmly. 'But tell me now, what brings you here? I have the distinct sensation, Gabriella, that this is not just a social call.'

'Well, actually, you're right.' Gabriella looked up, tried to muster a smile, then gave up. Instead she raised her palms in the air and dropped them in her lap. 'It's all a disaster, Madame.'

'What is a disaster? Explain.'

'My marriage. You must have seen the papers?'

'Actually, no. What papers? I live here in

Switzerland and do not read all the foreign press, you know.'

'Of course not. I forgot. But it is all over the British and American press. On the front page.'

'What is?' Madame asked patiently.

'Him—with her.'

'"Him" being who, Gabriella? Please express yourself clearly,' she admonished, in the reprimanding tone Gabriella remembered well. 'I am failing to follow you.'

'My husband—the Prince. He was photographed kissing his mistress. It's on the front page of every tabloid. Oh, I won't go back, Madame. I refuse to,' she said, tears burning her eyes as she jumped up and paced the room.

'Now, calm down, *mon enfant*. You are telling me that your husband has been pictured kissing another woman and it is splattered all over the newspapers?'

'Exactly.' Gabriella whirled around. 'You do see why I couldn't stay, don't you, Madame? I thought of going back to Brazil but—well, there are reasons why I don't want to go on a long journey just now.'

'I see. So that is why you came back to school?'

'Yes. I loved it here. I was happy. I need time to think. Oh, would it be all right if I stayed a little? I have nowhere else to go, except to some hotel—and that would be awful right now.'

'But of course you can stay, *cherie*,' the headmistress said in soothing tones, rising and taking Gabriella's hands in hers. 'You can have Mademoiselle Choiseul's old room. Nobody is using it at the moment. But, Gabriella, tell me the whole truth. It is not like you to run from adversity. I would be less surprised if I'd heard that you'd had a terrible row about the incident with him.'

'Perhaps under other circumstances I would have,' she agreed with a little laugh. 'But you see, I've changed, Madame. Ricardo only married me because my father asked him to on his deathbed. He stays with me and is courteous and kind and—oh, so many things,' she said, gulping and turning away. 'But the truth is this marriage is nothing more than an obligation for him. He was with this woman long before he met me. In a way she has more right to him than I do.'

'I see,' Madame replied, reading between the lines far more than Gabriella was consciously saying. 'And what do you think the future will bring?'

'I think we shall separate, and then in two years we can ask for a divorce. Only…'

'Only what, *ma chère*? Please open up and tell me the whole truth. You will feel better, and together we will be able to seek a solution to the problem.'

'Well, I'm finding it hard to believe myself, because we only made—that is, we haven't been very close,' she said, blushing, 'but I'm expecting a baby.'

'Oh, *ma chère enfant*. Now I understand your affliction,' Madame responded sympathetically. 'Still, this is wonderful news, Gabriella.' She drew the girl back onto the high-backed Louis XV brocade chair and sat down opposite.

'I wish it were. I mean, part of me is thrilled to think that I have life inside me. But then I think of the future—a life without love, Ricardo coming and going, not knowing where he is or with whom, worrying the whole time, being made to look like a fool when everyone around us will know that he has a mistress or several other women. I don't think I could bear it,' she said, her throat strangled as she dropped her head. 'I don't think I could stand that kind of life. It's not what I dreamt of in a marriage.'

'No. I understand you very well, and I think you are absolutely right. That is no way to conduct matrimony. But are you sure he really loves this other woman?'

'Yes. I've seen them together. They're intimate. You can just tell.'

'I see. That, of course, is a problem. Have you told him about the child?'

'No.' Gabriella shook her head fiercely. 'I haven't said a word. Oh, I know he would be wonderfully kind and caring, and I would be surrounded by every comfort. But that's not what I want from him. I—' She turned away once more, stifling the tears, and Madame Delorme watched her carefully.

'Gabriella, do you mind if I ask you a personal question?'

'No,' she gulped. 'Go ahead.'

'Do you love your husband?'

Gabriella hesitated a moment, then her head came round and her eyes met the older woman's. 'Yes,' she answered truthfully, squashing the pain that the word caused her. 'Yes, I do. I know it seems crazy, when we were married in such a hurry and against our wills, but I do love him—which is why I have to leave him, or I'll make both our lives a living hell.'

'I see.' Madame Delorme sat thoughtfully for a moment. Then, briskly, she got up. '*Bien*, let's go and install you in your room now. After you're settled you'll feel better.' She smiled encouragingly and Gabriella got up.

Together they left the sitting room and headed up the stairs. The bell had just rung, and girls were pouring out of classrooms. Some of the younger ones recognised her and came up to chat. But even as she felt a wave of nostalgia at not being a part of this life any longer, Gabriella quickly realised that she had moved on. She was now in a different phase of her existence. One she had to deal with as an adult.

With a sigh, she followed Madame Delorme down the passage to the room that had used to belong to Mademoiselle Choiseul, the French teacher. At least here she could stop for a while and think. And make plans for what right now struck her as a bleak future.

Once back in her office Madame Delorme sat thoughtfully behind her elegant French antique desk. Gabriella was in a fix, and this situation could not be allowed to endure. It went against the grain, but, just as she often had to take decisions with her pupils, Madame knew it was her duty to take a decision now. Reluctantly she reached for her telephone book. She would ring her old friend the Contessa Elizabetta. Perhaps by putting their heads together they would come up with something.

'Hello—Elizabetta?'

'Yes. Is that you, Marianne?'

'Yes. How pleasing of you to recognise my voice.'

'Of course I do. How would I not recognise one of my oldest and dearest friends? Tell me, how are things?'

'Fine. But, actually, I'm calling about a slight problem that indirectly concerns you.'

'Oh?'

'Well, I have Gabriella here.'

'Oh, thank God for that!' the Contessa exclaimed. 'Ricardo will be so thankful. He's been looking for her everywhere. We knew she was headed for Switzerland. It should have occurred to me she might have gone to you. We've been going out of our minds, trying to think where she could have run to, poor child, after that awful display of vulgarity in the papers. It is unbelievable what the press will stoop to.'

'It is also unbelievable what a recently married man will stoop to,' Madame Delorme replied dryly.

'I know, I know,' the Contessa agreed with a sigh. 'But boys will be boys, you know. And unfortunately this marriage was not properly planned. Poor Gabriella. I feel so sorry for her, and wish she had come here if she felt she had to get away. We are trying to keep her absence quiet for the present— though of course the press are all over the place, trying to get more salacious titbits for their readers. But I am so worried about her. Is she all right?'

'Yes and no. I am worried about her. She looks far too thin and worn out, poor child. If I had the chance, I would haul your nephew over the coals for what he's done.'

'Oh, believe me, I already have. But, actually, I don't think things are quite as simple as they appear.'

'No?'

'No. I get the impression that this whole incident was a set-up—probably by the mistress. He assures me that he did not spend the night with her and that he had no intention of carrying on the relationship. That he told her so. She probably did this to take revenge. He did not spell it out in so many words, but I get the impression he is truly concerned and perhaps not a little in love with his wife—even if he doesn't know it himself yet.'

'Good. Well, we'll leave him to stew for a few days, *ma chère amie*, and then see what we can do to patch up this messy business.'

'I hate not telling him where she is, when he is obviously distraught with worry, but I do believe you may be right. Oh, Marianne, we are probably nothing but two old busybodies, but I would so like to see these two children happy. You know, I have an odd feeling that they really suit one another. Perhaps Gonzalo Guimaraes was right after all. He was a cunning old fox...and too handsome for his own good,' she said with a nostalgic sigh.

'Very well. Then I shall keep you informed.'

'Yes, my dear. But don't eke this out for too long. You know how bad I am at keeping secrets.'

Madame Delorme laughed heartily. Ever since they had been at boarding school themselves she'd known Elizabetta was a hopeless liar and could never keep a secret. 'I promise the suspense will not last too long. Just long enough for him to come to his senses. He's a man, after all, and if things are made too easy for men they don't appreciate it.'

CHAPTER TWELVE

THE phone rang and Ambrosia leaped on to it.

'Hello?'

'You saw yesterday's papers?' Ricardo's voice cut like a knife down the line.

'Yes, of course I did. It was awful. I can barely leave the flat. I can't think who did this. It's appalling.'

'Whoever it was, Ambrosia, I can assure you they will pay a high price for invading my privacy and trying to muck up my marriage.'

'Your marriage?' Ambrosia could not repress a smile of delight. 'You mean Gabriella saw the pictures? How awful. I'm so sorry, Ricky.'

There was a moment's hesitation. 'Thanks to this mischief my wife has left me. I have no idea where she is, and I am very worried about her. I hold you entirely to blame.'

'Me? But— '

'Don't play games, Ambrosia. I know how you operate when you want something. I've seen you in action before. I just never believed you'd stoop so low.' His voice rasped on her nerves, cold and unforgiving.

'But, Ricky, you have it all wrong. I was appalled. I tell you, I'm positively being invaded. I can't get the wretched press off my doorstep. I was thinking of coming to Maldoravia. After all, my villa there is very secluded and private. And at least that way we could see each other...'

'See each other? Are you completely mad? I forbid you to come anywhere near Maldoravia. As for seeing you, I sincerely hope that last night was the last time you'll ever cross my path.'

Ambrosia swallowed and her hands trembled. There was no disappointment in his voice, only icy fury. Her pulse raced. Had she played her cards wrong? she wondered, her heart sinking. But surely now that Gabriella was well out of the way—might even decide to leave him permanently—the coast would be clear, and after all this had died down he would change his mind. Yes, surely. This reaction was nothing but a natural passing phase.

'Okay, darling,' she said meekly. 'I'll do whatever you want.'

'Do not use that term of endearment ever again,' he hissed. 'Now, get the hell out of my life and stay out. You've done enough damage as it is, and I shall never forgive you.'

The phone went dead and she looked at it thoughtfully, wrinkling her nose. Strong words, of course, and the result of her handiwork was not great. But on the other hand it was to be expected that he would be angry. And serve him right, for leaving her on her own and running back to his little virgin wife. Once all the fuss died down she had no doubt that she would achieve her objective. Gabriella would probably make a scene, and that would annoy him. Little by little the couple would drift apart, and she would be there to pick up the pieces exactly as planned.

It sounded good, but Ambrosia was not quite as confident as she had been. She had a sinking feeling that she should not have allowed her temper to get the better of her.

For the first time she wondered if she would come out winning in the end.

'I've traced her,' Ricardo announced triumphantly, coming into the drawing room where Constanza and the Contessa were sitting having coffee.

'Really?' Constanza looked up, excited. 'Oh, I'm so glad, Ricky. I've been so worried. Where is she?'

'Apparently she's in Switzerland. My people tracked down the driver of the limo. She had the car drop her off at the Beau Rivage Hotel in Lausanne, but she's not registered there. I had the concierge check. And there is no one who matches her description in the hotel. Even under another name.'

'Very strange,' the Contessa murmured vaguely. 'Ricardo, have some coffee.'

'In a moment, Aunt,' he said, his eyes narrowing. 'Aunt Elizabetta, I don't suppose you would know anything about her whereabouts? If I recall correctly, you are very friendly with Gabriella's old headmistress, from her school in Switzerland. I remember you talking about her not that long ago. Perhaps you have an idea of where she might be?'

'Me? How would I know?' she spluttered, almost dropping the coffee pot. 'Now look what you've made me do, Ricky,' she exclaimed, placing the coffee pot back down on the tray and fussing over a spot on the cloth.

Constanza and Ricardo exchanged a look. They knew their aunt well.

'Aunt Elizabetta, if you know anything—anything at all—you must tell Ricky,' Constanza said, looking her aunt full in the eyes.

'Well, I...'

'Please, Aunt.' Ricardo came over quickly and, sitting down, took her hands in his. 'You have no idea how important this is. If she has confided in you, if you know anything at all, you must tell me at once. Our whole future could be at stake.'

'Well, after the way you've behaved I really don't see what future you have with Gabriella,' his aunt countered, regaining some of her composure.

'Look, I had nothing to do with that picture or those articles. It was some busybody reporter who happened to be spying on us. It was foolish of me to go out in public with Ambrosia, but the photo was just a piece of bad luck.'

'Are you sure?' Constanza got up and, turning her back to the window, leaned against the sill. 'Are you sure you weren't set up, Ricky?'

'By whom?'

'By Ambrosia herself.'

'It's possible,' he conceded slowly.

'It all strikes me as far too pat to be just a coincidence. I mean, who knew you were going to dine at Mark's? And all those details about Ruddy and Gabriella and the accident. You said you had no intention of having an amorous evening with the woman. Try and remember the circumstances. Did you kiss her out of the blue or did she conveniently kiss you?'

Ricardo dropped his aunt's hands and rose. He remained silent for a long moment, then turned and faced his sister.

'I've been a fool,' he said quietly. 'But I've already made it quite clear to Ambrosia that it's over between us. If she thinks otherwise, she's the fool.'

'I won't contradict you on either,' Constanza replied in a sisterly manner. 'I think she set the whole thing up to create a rift between you and Gabriella. Now, Aunt Elizabetta, spill the beans and tell us the truth. Gabriella's gone back to her school, hasn't she?'

'Yes. You are right. She went to seek out the one person she felt she could trust—my old friend Marianne Delorme, her headmistress.'

'And she's there at the school now?' Ricardo insisted.

'Apparently so. I believe Marianne is very upset with you. It seems Gabriella is unhappy and barely eats. You have a lot to answer for, Ricky. You had no right to marry that child and behave the way you have. I am positively ashamed of you.'

'That I am very well aware of,' he said bitterly. 'But this last episode was not of my making. Ambrosia will pay dearly for her tricks.'

'Right now, I wouldn't worry about her,' Constanza replied.

'I'm on my way to Lausanne,' Ricardo answered, with a smile in her direction. 'I'm so relieved that I've finally discovered Gabriella's whereabouts. How long did you plan to keep this a secret, Aunt? I can't believe you didn't tell me.'

'It serves you jolly well right,' Aunt Elizabetta replied firmly. 'You don't deserve her, the way you go on. And I'm not speaking just of this newspaper incident. You know very well what I mean.'

'I can assure you, *madame*, that from now on things will be different.'

'So I should hope,' she replied with a sniff as he left the room, leaving the door swinging behind him.

'So. Elizabetta let the cat out of the bag, did she?' Madame Delorme said as Ricardo entered the sitting room and the maid closed the door quietly behind him.

'No. Actually I traced her through the car company, then confronted my aunt. I remembered your close friendship and put two and two together, *madame*,' he said, raising her hand to his lips.

Madame Delorme eyed him askance. The man was more charming than she had imagined. No wonder Gabriella was in love. But still, she had no inclination to facilitate his task. 'And so you arrive here on my doorstep, without so much as a by-your-leave,' she said, in a tone that would have had her pupils quaking in their shoes, 'and expect your wife to be awaiting you?'

'Not at all. *Madame*, you must excuse the precipitous manner of my arrival. As soon as I knew of Gabriella's whereabouts I came at once. You must realise how worried I was about my wife.'

'Good. You deserve to be worried after the way you've behaved.'

Ricardo cleared his throat. He was not used to being treated like an errant schoolboy.

'I have come to relieve you of the responsibility for her,' he said in a grand manner.

'*Vraiment*, Your Royal Highness?' she replied, raising an amused and critical brow. 'Well, that is all very well. But who says that your Gabriella wants to see you?'

'*Madame*, I must insist. Gabriella is my wife. She has an obligation to see me.'

'You know, if I was you I would alter my approach,' Madame said in a pleasant tone, sitting down on the stiff-backed brocade sofa and crossing her legs. 'You may sit down. We need to talk this matter over sensibly.'

Ricardo sat opposite. It was the first time in many years that he had felt out of his element.

'I assure you, *madame*, that I want nothing more than to recover my wife and take her home, where she belongs.'

'Your Highness, Gabriella is not an object that you can bundle up and take with you. She is a very sensitive and hurt young woman who is suffering the deep humiliation of having been made a fool of in front of the world. Apart from anything else, she is not well.'

'Not well? What is wrong with her?'

'Among other things, unhappiness. It is an illness that can do much harm. And you, young man, are to blame for this state of affairs.'

'*Madame*, please,' he pleaded with a smile. 'I know I'm in the wrong, but I beg you to believe me when

I tell you that things are not at all as they appear. It seems that I was set up. I suppose that my friend—'

'You mean your mistress?'

'Uh, *ex*-mistress.' He regained his composure and continued smoothly, 'She perhaps thought that if she could separate me from Gabriella and create a rift I would return to her. I don't know. Suffice it to say that I have made it abundantly clear to her that whatever there was between us is definitively over.' He got up, raised his hands, then let them drop. 'All I know is I need to see my wife as soon as possible and explain to her what happened. I can't allow her to go on thinking that I…'

'That you?'

'That I betrayed her.'

'Well, I think you may find her a little difficult to convince. After all, the evidence is staring her in the face.'

'All I'm asking is a chance to talk to her.'

Madame eyed him, then she sighed. 'I suppose you're right. At some point you will both have to come to terms with the situation—face one another and clear this matter up. But I'm afraid right now that is impossible.'

'Why?' he asked, raising a haughty brow.

'Because Gabriella is not here. She is at the doctor's.'

'The doctor? Is she ill?' His expression changed immediately to one of concern and Madame felt relieved. Perhaps he did care far more for Gabriella than she had at first thought.

'Well, not exactly. She…'

'*Madame*, I demand that you tell me the truth about my wife's state of health.'

Madame Delorme hesitated. She hated interfering. On the other hand, she knew how stubborn Gabriella could be—and proud. At last she took a decision.

'This goes against the grain, and I would not normally betray a confidence.' She sighed. 'But I think it is for the well-being of you both. I do it on one condition, though.'

'Which is?'

'That you do not tell Gabriella that you know. Let her tell you herself.'

'Very well,' he said, mystified. 'But please, *madame*, whatever it is, I have to know.'

'I have your word?'

'Absolutely. My solemn promise that whatever you tell me I will keep to myself until she sees fit to tell me.'

'Do not be surprised if that takes a little time.'

'Fine,' he said impatiently. 'But what is it?'

'Gabriella is expecting a baby.'

'What?' Ricardo stopped dead in his tracks.

'Yes. There is nothing surprising in that, surely?'

'No. Yes. What I mean is... Oh, my God, what a mess.' He sat down abruptly. 'Is she okay? No, she isn't, is she? That's why she was so pale. Oh, God, what a mess I've made of things.'

'Well, it's too late to cry over spilt milk,' Madame pointed out in a matter-of-fact tone. 'The main thing is that you must be there for her from now on.'

'When will she be back?'

'In about half an hour. Now, I'm afraid I'm rather

busy,' she said, looking at her watch, 'but you're welcome to wait here.'

'Thank you, *madame*.'

'I shall tell my secretary to advise Gabriella to come to my sitting room the minute she gets in. And,' she added looking at him with a touch of humour, 'make sure you don't botch this up. It may be a one-time opportunity.'

With that she exited the room, leaving Ricardo to pace impatiently up and down, her words ringing in his ears.

'Gabriella, you're wanted in Madame Delorme's sitting room,' Katie the secretary said as Gabriella came into the hall.

'I'll go right away.'

Gabriella, her hair pulled back in a ponytail and wearing jeans and a white shirt, looked like any one of the students as she walked across the hall and knocked on the door of Madame Delorme's sitting room. To her surprise she heard a male voice answer. She frowned, but turned the door handle anyway, then stopped, rooted to the ground, when she saw Ricardo standing in the middle of the room, tall, serious and handsome in a light grey suit.

'Gabriella,' he said, moving towards her and taking her hands in his before she could react. 'I have been so worried about you, *cara mia*, you have no idea.'

'Oh, I think I do,' she said, regaining her balance and wrenching her hands from his grip. 'If the papers are anything to go by, I have an excellent perception of exactly how worried you are.'

'Please, you must let me explain.'

'Don't waste your time,' she said haughtily, taking a quick step back. 'There is nothing you can say to justify that. Frankly, I'm glad you've come. At least now we can talk and clear the air. Ever since we married you have been wishing you were with her,' she said, her head held high. 'Well, now there is nothing to stop you. She was what you wanted all along.'

'You're wrong. I—'

'I know our marriage was not fair on you,' Gabriella interrupted, determined to have her say, 'and that my father forced you into it. Also I know that you and Ambrosia are having a long-standing affair. I suppose you thought I would simply turn my eyes the other way while you carried on your relationship with her? Well, I won't. I won't be made a laughing stock. I won't go through the humiliation of my husband being unfaithful to me.'

'Is that all you care about? That people will laugh behind your back?' His eyes narrowed and he drew himself up to his full height.

'Of course. I refuse to be the victim of such humiliation.'

'Is that all you feel, Gabriella? Humiliation? Shame?'

'I don't know what you mean,' she said, turning away, her lip quivering.

'I mean, Gabriella, that you know as well as I do that when we made love it was not just a coming together of two married people. It was special. It was magical.'

She stopped dead at his words and swallowed. A shudder ran through her.

'Gabriella, I have made love to many women in my time. I believe I can honestly consider myself an experienced lover,' he said with a rueful touch of humour. 'But when you and I made love I felt something I had never felt before.'

'If that was the case,' she said in small voice, 'why were you kissing the woman you've been making love to for the past couple of years?'

'It was a set-up.'

'Yeah, right,' she muttered, clenching her fists. 'You know, I may look stupid, but actually I'm not. You were kissing her, and,' she added as a clincher, turning on him, her eyes flashing with emerald anger, 'you looked as if you were enjoying it. Did you have a pleasant night together, I wonder?' She stopped herself, swallowed once more, and shook her head. 'Oh, God. This is exactly what I wanted to avoid. Ricardo, you must understand…' she said, her anger fading as she sank onto a chair and unconsciously placed her hand on her tummy. 'I know you have had many women—I've read about you for years in the press. I can't expect you to give up your lifestyle; it wouldn't be fair when this is nothing but a marriage of convenience for you. But please understand that I could never live with you under those conditions. I couldn't bear it. I—'

'Why not?' he insisted, looking down at her, a new and intent gleam in his eye. 'Why couldn't you bear it? If for you our marriage is only an obligation, what do you care what I do?'

'Because I...'

'Because you have deeper feelings for me than you want to admit?' he challenged, drawing her up and into his arms, his hand snaking behind her head and forcing it back so that she was obliged to meet his eyes full-on.

'No! I—'

'Don't lie to me, Gabriella. I thought perhaps it was just I who felt those things when we made love, that for you it was just a first experience and you had let me teach you. But now I want the truth.'

'Why should I tell you of my feelings?' she whispered, her eyes holding his.

'Because I love you,' he said. 'And I want to know if you love me.'

She let out a little gasp and her heart leaped. 'How can you say that when—?'

'Oh, forget about that damn picture. It was all Ambrosia, playing her silly tricks. I've told her it is over—completely over. And, for the record, I did not spend the night with her.'

'Oh.' Gabriella swallowed, wanting to believe him.

'But I need to know the truth,' Ricardo insisted. 'Do you love me?'

'Yes,' she whispered at last, letting her head sink onto his chest. 'Yes, I love you, Ricardo. Which is why I can't stay with you. Because although you say now that you love me, I think you're just trying to make me feel better. There will be other women and—'

'Will you stop talking this damn nonsense, *cara*? Do you know that this is the first time I have ever said to any woman that I love her?' He gave her shoulders a little shake and smiled down into her eyes. 'Oh, my beautiful, wonderful girl. Gonzalo was a clever man. He realised far more than you or I ever could have, and I shall be eternally grateful to him for having forced our hands.'

He pulled her close and, sitting down, drew her onto his knee. 'Now, tell me, my love. Is it just *mal d'amour* that has been making you feel ill the past few days, or is there something else? I swear, I will never let you go through anything like this again as long as you live, my love.'

Gabriella let her head lean against his shoulder. She could hardly believe what was happening. She felt so wonderfully happy in his arms, so warm and secure, so filled with excitement and desire for him as they touched. But was it just an illusion? Had he really told Ambrosia that it was over for good? She looked up into his eyes. Could she trust him?

Then Ricardo turned her face up to his and his lips came down on hers. Her body tensed, her heart soared, and her whole being melted as his hands coursed over her.

After taking their leave of Madame Delorme, Gabriella and Ricardo drove to the Beau Rivage Hotel. They were shown to a sumptuous suite overlooking the lake.

'Come, my love, we have a lot to catch up on,' Ricardo said, once the bellboy and the manager had disappeared.

Gabriella hesitated. There was so much to tell him,

so much she needed to confide, but she needed to be completely sure first. Could not just take the leap.

'Ricardo, are you sure of everything you said to me earlier? Do you swear that you told Ambrosia it was over between you?' she questioned, looping her arms around his neck and feeling his hands caress her rib-cage, feeling that same searing heat running through her, making logic fade and her feelings come alive.

'You don't believe me?'

'I want to believe you.'

'Good. Because I have many defects, but being a liar is not one of them,' he said, an edge to his voice. 'I have been very cruel with you, my darling, and I deserve any mistrust that you have of me. All I can tell you is that there is no cause for you to be upset or worried any longer. Ambrosia,' he added coldly, 'has cooked her goose.'

This last broke the tension, and Gabriella laughed heartily. 'What a wonderful expression,' she exclaimed.

'Well, it sums it up nicely. I never want to lay eyes on her again. If she had tried to hurt me, I would have understood. But I will never allow anyone to hurt you or our—'

'Or our what?'

'Or anything to do with you,' he countered.

Gabriella frowned. For a moment she'd thought he was going to say *our child*. She hesitated a moment, then looked once more into his eyes. All she read there was deep enduring love and sincerity. It was time, she realised, to tell him the truth.

'Ricardo, whatever happens between us, there is something you need to know,' she said at last.

'Then tell me.'

'I—I'm going to have your baby.'

'My darling.' He took her in his arms and gazed down into her eyes. 'I was wondering how long it would take you to trust me enough to tell me.'

'You knew?'

'I wangled it out of poor Madame Delorme.'

'You are something, aren't you?' she exclaimed, shaking her head.

'I'm yours, Gabriella, for now and ever more. Do you believe that, my darling?'

'I want to,' she responded, with a little smile curving her lips.

'Then let me prove it to you.'

Before she could protest Ricardo was slipping off her shirt, her jeans, her bra and panties, letting them fall in a pile on the oriental rug. Seconds later he was naked too, taking her into his arms, drawing her close against him, making her feel the intenseness of his desire. Then they were on the huge bed, Gabriella thrown back amongst the pillows, her hair tossed wildly, while Ricardo introduced her to new and wondrous sensations that she had not known existed. As his tongue traced a pattern down her throat, flicking her taut breasts then heading south until he reached her core, she thought she could bear it no longer. Her fingers dragged through his hair and she arched, feeling his tongue flick her in the most sensitive of spots. Then came a long shuddering release such as she had never known.

Just as she was coming to grips with the over-whelming experience, he moved above her. Pinning his arms on either side of her, he entered her, hard and fast. 'I will never let you go, my love, my beautiful wife. Not now or ever.'

She could not reply. Her eyes were riveted to his and her legs came up about his waist as together they fell into a fast, passionate rhythm. Gabriella thought it was impossible to come again after what she'd already experienced. But suddenly the rhythm changed, and all at once Ricardo threw back his head, let out a groan, and she a cry, and together they tumbled into a wave of delight among the rumpled sheets.

Later they sat on the terrace of the hotel's Rotonde restaurant, overlooking the gardens and Lake Geneva. Dusk was beginning to fall, but as they sipped champagne and held hands they could still see the pedalo boats on the water and the lights of Evian starting to glimmer on the French side of the lake.

'It is beautiful,' Gabriella said with a sigh.

'No more beautiful than knowing that at last we are one.'

Gabriella looked across at him. There was some-thing new, something wonderful in his expression that hadn't been there before.

'I know, my darling,' she replied. 'I love you. And from now on I shall trust you from the bottom of my heart.'

'Thank God for that,' he responded, bringing his lips down on hers, 'because I have no intention of letting you go. Not now or ever.'

HARLEQUIN® Presents®

**The world's bestselling romance series...
The series that brings you your favorite authors,
month after month:**

Helen Bianchin...Emma Darcy
Lynne Graham...Penny Jordan
Miranda Lee...Sandra Marton
Anne Mather...Carole Mortimer
Susan Napier...Michelle Reid

and many more uniquely talented authors!

Wealthy, powerful, gorgeous men...
Women who have feelings just like your own...
The stories you love, set in exotic, glamorous locations...

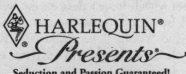

HARLEQUIN® Presents®

Seduction and Passion Guaranteed!

HARLEQUIN *Presents*

We've captured a royal slice of life

By Royal Command

Kings, counts, dukes and princes…

Don't miss these stories of charismatic kings,
commanding counts, demanding dukes and
playboy princes. Read all about their privileged
lives, love affairs…even their scandals!

Let us treat you like a queen—
relax and enjoy our regal miniseries.

THE ITALIAN
DUKE'S WIFE
by Penny Jordan

Italian Lorenzo, Duce di Montesavro, chooses English
tourist Jodie Oliver to be his convenient wife. But when
he unleashes within Jodie a desire she never knew she
possessed, he regrets his no-consummation rule.…

On sale April 2006.